The  rolls

A 'el

(Matt Drake #36)

By David Leadbeater

Copyright © 2025 by David Leadbeater

ISBN: 9798308090113

All rights reserved.
No part of this publication may be reproduced, distributed, or transmitted in any form or by any means, including photocopying, recording, or other electronic or mechanical methods, without the prior written permission of the publisher/author except in the case of brief quotations embodied in critical reviews and certain other non-commercial uses permitted by copyright law.
All characters in this book are fictitious, and any resemblance to actual persons living or dead is purely coincidental.

Classification: Thriller, adventure, action, mystery, suspense, archaeological, military, historical, assassination, terrorism, assassin, spy

Other Books by David Leadbeater:

Blood Requiem

The Matt Drake Series
A constantly evolving, action-packed romp based in the escapist action-adventure genre:

The Bones of Odin (Matt Drake #1)
The Blood King Conspiracy (Matt Drake #2)
The Gates of Hell (Matt Drake 3)
The Tomb of the Gods (Matt Drake #4)
Brothers in Arms (Matt Drake #5)
The Swords of Babylon (Matt Drake #6)
Blood Vengeance (Matt Drake #7)
Last Man Standing (Matt Drake #8)
The Plagues of Pandora (Matt Drake #9)
The Lost Kingdom (Matt Drake #10)
The Ghost Ships of Arizona (Matt Drake #11)
The Last Bazaar (Matt Drake #12)
The Edge of Armageddon (Matt Drake #13)
The Treasures of Saint Germain (Matt Drake #14)
Inca Kings (Matt Drake #15)
The Four Corners of the Earth (Matt Drake #16)
The Seven Seals of Egypt (Matt Drake #17)
Weapons of the Gods (Matt Drake #18)
The Blood King Legacy (Matt Drake #19)
Devil's Island (Matt Drake #20)
The Fabergé Heist (Matt Drake #21)
Four Sacred Treasures (Matt Drake #22)
The Sea Rats (Matt Drake #23)
Blood King Takedown (Matt Drake #24)
Devil's Junction (Matt Drake #25)

Voodoo soldiers (Matt Drake #26)
The Carnival of Curiosities (Matt Drake #27)
Theatre of War (Matt Drake #28)
Shattered Spear (Matt Drake #29)
Ghost Squadron (Matt Drake #30)
A Cold Day in Hell (Matt Drake #31)
The Winged Dagger (Matt Drake #32)
Two Minutes to Midnight (Matt Drake #33)
The Devil's Reaper (Matt Drake#34)
The Dark Tsar (Matt Drake #35)

The Alicia Myles Series
Aztec Gold (Alicia Myles #1)
Crusader's Gold (Alicia Myles #2)
Caribbean Gold (Alicia Myles #3)
Chasing Gold (Alicia Myles #4)
Galleon's Gold (Alicia Myles #5)
Hawaiian Gold (Alicia Myles #6)

The Torsten Dahl Thriller Series
Stand Your Ground (Dahl Thriller #1)

The Relic Hunters Series
The Relic Hunters (Relic Hunters #1)
The Atlantis Cipher (Relic Hunters #2)
The Amber Secret (Relic Hunters #3)
The Hostage Diamond (Relic Hunters #4)
The Rocks of Albion (Relic Hunters #5)
The Illuminati Sanctum (Relic Hunters #6)
The Illuminati Endgame (Relic Hunters #7)
The Atlantis Heist (Relic Hunters #8)

The City of a Thousand Ghosts (Relic Hunters #9)
Hierarchy of Madness (Relic Hunters #10)
The Contest (Relic Hunters #11)
The Maestro's Treasure (Relic Hunters #12)

The Joe Mason Series
The Vatican Secret (Joe Mason #1)
The Demon Code (Joe Mason #2)
The Midnight Conspiracy (Joe Mason #3)
The Babylon Plot (Joe Mason #4)
The Traitor's Gold (Joe Mason #5)
The Angel Deception (Joe Mason #6)

The Rogue Series
Rogue (Book One)

The Disavowed Series:
The Razor's Edge (Disavowed #1)
In Harm's Way (Disavowed #2)
Threat Level: Red (Disavowed #3)

The Chosen Few Series
Chosen (The Chosen Trilogy #1)
Guardians (The Chosen Trilogy #2)
Heroes (The Chosen Trilogy #3)

Short Stories
Walking with Ghosts (A short story)
A Whispering of Ghosts (A short story)

All genuine comments are very welcome at:

davidleadbeater2011@hotmail.co.uk

Twitter: @dleadbeater2011

Visit David's website for the latest news and information:
davidleadbeater.com

The Hellhound Scrolls

THE HELLHOUND SCROLLS

CHAPTER ONE

The wind hit the house like wailing demons, screaming and shrieking, threatening to tear it from its very foundations.

Lily sat still in bed, with the covers drawn over her head. The room was dark. The curtains were drawn. Shivers ran through her frame. The monster was getting closer and closer. Any moment now, it would reach down for her through the darkness.

It was after midnight, her parents long since gone to bed to catch whatever fitful sleep they may get. Lily didn't expect to get any sleep, but she *did* expect to get eaten sometime soon.

The behemoth was obviously approaching, getting louder and louder. The entire house shook as the gusts hit time after time. The noise was like an express train she'd once heard bellowing by. She'd been too close, and it had terrified her. She shook under the covers, alternately hot and cold. The minutes passed like oozing molasses. This was like nothing she had ever experienced before. It was something many people had never experienced before.

According to her parents, it was a *typhoon,* and it was *very unlikely* to hit Singapore. Well, that didn't help her now, caught in the heart of it. Except this wasn't the heart of it, they'd said. That would be calm. This was very much the leading edge.

It battered her home on the beach, made her feel small. A rectangular picture on the wall juddered and fell askew. A lamp shook its way across the bedside table, making her catch it before it fell to the ground. She'd thought about turning it on, creating light to ward off the deafening dark, but couldn't bring herself to do it. The ear-splitting howling went on and on, and it made her feel like the smallest person in the world.

Glass rattled. A small ornament fell off a shelf, thudding to the floor. Lily heard it, she didn't see it. The covers were her only comfort. No, that wasn't true. She had a bear under there with her too, an off-white, tousled little guy called Bernie. She hugged Bernie. The bear hugged her back, comforting her.

Lily closed her eyes. The noise and the rattling didn't go away. It was getting worse, escalating. Through the thin walls, Lily heard her parents talking, and then they shouted to her, asking if she was okay. Lily stayed brave and shouted back that she was fine even as she went hot and cold through fear. She had Bernie. That was enough.

They lived close to the beach. They were right in the typhoon's track. It was hitting hard, but her parents had assured her their house was solid, and no evacuation instruction had been ordered. Lily was surprised, because it felt like an immense monster was eating her entire neighbourhood alive.

She clutched Bernie as the nightmare continued. The trouble was – there was nowhere she could go, nothing she could do. It was just her and the elements, and they kept her alive on a whim. She could hear something banging on the roof above. Was it a tile? Something else? Something that had been scooped up by the wind and then caught by her roof?

A particularly heavy gust blasted the window. Lily could bear it no longer under the covers. She threw them off, stared around her darkened room. Everything was as it should be, except the little ornament that had fallen off and the askew painting. This was good. This showed that, despite the monster, all was okay and it wasn't getting in. She brought Bernie out of the covers too, held him in her arms, staring into the dark. Her eyes were accustomed to it, and now she turned her head towards the covered window.

It was out there, screaming. It was smashing the coastline, churning up the waves, scouring the beach where she often played. The thing was emotionless, cold, impervious. It didn't care what it destroyed, who it hurt, and yes, it would hurt someone tonight. It would do a lot of damage.

Lily stared at the curtains. Despite everything, they weren't moving, not a millimetre. It seemed unreal, considering the madness happening just inches away. It also made Lily feel that bit more secure. A thought occurred to her, summoning up her rebellious side. Dare she? It was a scary thought, and it made her insides curdle. But it also appealed to her. She was safe inside here... wasn't she?

Before she knew what she was doing, Lily had slipped out of bed. Her bare toes touched the familiar carpet. She scrunched them. Her arms grasped the little bear.

And then she took one step forward.

Everything howled. There was no respite from the storm. It pounded and it thrashed, venting its fury. Lily stood amid it all, and then she took another step. She was now two steps closer to the window, and nothing terrible had happened. A wave of courage surged through her.

Another step, and then a fourth. She was halfway across her room. This was no-man's-land; where anything could happen. She paused in her tracks, going still. Not a muscle moved. Bernie lay still in her arms. The typhoon pummelled the house and the beach beyond, and then something random clattered across their little garden.

Lily froze some more. The object passed by and nothing else was heard. The winds assaulted the night. She took a tentative step and then another and then found herself close to the curtains. She had made several small steps, but now she had come to the big one. The storm thrashed just beyond. Lily reached out, touched the dark material. She grasped it in one hand and paused.

Don't go near the window.

Her father's voice, spoken earlier that day when he had been prepping her for the night to come. She recalled it now. But she was brave; she had come this far. Each step made the next one easier. The curtains were held in her hand. She took a deep breath.

And a crash echoed through the house as something smashed against the walls. Lily froze in place. Her heart hammered so hard she thought it might burst. Had the monster come to call? She waited in place for what seemed like an hour, just unmoving, her hand touching the curtains. Bernie said nothing; he seemed to have no preferences either way. After a while, when no more crashing sounds came, she twitched open the curtains, drew them all the way back.

And gasped. The night was well lit by a full moon that shone brightly through scudding clouds. She could see her front garden, the narrow road beyond, the wide expanse of the beach beyond that. The streetlights were still on, creating further illumination. The first thing she saw were trees being whipped, the slender ones bent almost double. Their branches sliced at the air like long knives being manipulated by a giant. The beach was being scoured, its sands churning and whirling. The waves beyond that were boiling, rolling and thrashing against each other, running incessantly up the beach. The monster itself was invisible, no sign of the creator of all the chaos. Lily just saw a blurry pandemonium, a turmoil that might have been caused by the Devil.

She watched, feeling slightly better as she came face to face with the beast. She saw a plastic chair roll past, taking flight, and then hitting the ground before lifting off again. A trampoline tumbled by, deadly if it struck a pedestrian, but then who would be out in this? The winds creased the window, bending it slightly. Lily watched in fascination. Her eyes strayed further out, away, towards the beach and the roiling sea beyond.

It was beyond wild out there; the typhoon

concentrating much of its effort a mile or so to the west. Lily fancied she could see mountains for waves and that there were endless gusts and blasts of air, constant fury. She held Bernie up so that he could see it too, and the bear didn't seem to mind.

Lily felt strong. Tomorrow, at school, if it went ahead, she would tell all her friends about her bravery and she hoped they might have done something similar. Faced their fears. Stood up to the monster.

Lily squinted. What was this? She couldn't quite believe what she was seeing. From the far darkness, out at sea, a deeper darkness appeared to be approaching. It was an odd sight. It was huge. Were her eyes deceiving her?

She shook her head, blinked three times. Then she tried to focus. She was *certain* a darkness was approaching across the seas towards the beach. Could there in fact be a demon, a monster that brought the storm? Was this it? Lily almost bolted then, almost headed back for the bedcovers, but the thick darkness moved slowly and with purpose – it wasn't attacking her, or anything. It just *came on*.

Lily watched. The enormous patch of darkness came out of the shadows and approached the beach. It gained shape. It was like a stealth vessel, creeping inexorably forward. Finally, Lily could bear it no more.

'Mum! Dad! Come here. Hurry!'

Instantly, she heard movement through the walls. Seconds later, her parents burst into her room, eyes wild.

'What is it?' her dad cried. 'Are you okay? Why are you standing by the window?'

Lily just pointed. She stepped back slightly so they could see. They came up to her and peered into the chaotic night.

'What the hell *is* that?' her dad said.

Lily watched. The large shape sidled through the seas, storm-tossed, and then hit the beach at speed. It slinked along the sands, urged by the incessantly incoming waters, approaching the line of houses with a grand majesty. It slowed and slowed, and then stopped, remaining upright, itself now struck by the raging winds.

'Am I really seeing this?' her father asked.

Lily knew the shape. She knew what she was looking at. But she really couldn't believe her eyes. 'What is it?' she asked.

'It's a ship. A galleon,' her mother replied.

'But where's it come from?' Lily said. 'It looks old.'

Her father took a deep breath. 'From the depths,' he said softly. 'It's been dragged up from the bottom of the sea.'

CHAPTER TWO

Kerry Roberts ran a hand through her short-cropped blonde hair and looked several thousand feet down, out of the plane's window. Singapore lay sprawled out below, and her eyes travelled inexorably towards the coastline, her eventual destination.

The plane banked and then levelled out before starting to descend. Kerry was a seasoned traveller and leaned back, closing her eyes. Maybe she could grab a couple of winks as the plane took its time to come in for its landing. Quickly, she checked the chunky watch that adorned her left wrist. Late morning. She would have plenty of time to get to the site today for a preliminary look around.

Kerry was a forthright, straight-talking, knowledgeable archaeologist, respected in her field. She'd lost count of the number of jobs like this she'd been sent on, but she enjoyed visiting different parts of the world, and she loved her job. She worked indirectly for a well-respected firm attached to the Natural History Museum of New York, who had contacts in governments all over the world. When those governments felt they needed a little seasoned help... they called her firm.

As the plane came into land, her thoughts turned

as they regularly did to her dad. She missed him every day, and thought about him often, wondering what he'd do in any particular situation. When the plane touched down, it jolted her out of her reverie, bringing her back to the present. Soon, she was deplaning and then queuing up to get through security, and next she was waiting for her suitcase.

Kerry was in her hotel room an hour later, and then looking for something quick to eat. She hadn't eaten in hours, not enjoying plane food. She found a local spot and something that looked normal, sat down and ate it. By now, it was mid-afternoon, and she was almost out of time, but decided even if she only had an hour, it was worth visiting the site today.

She flagged down a cab and gave the driver the address, directing him to a suburb on the coast. The driver nodded resignedly, as if he'd already been out that way several times today. She sat back in the baking car and looked at the passing sights, seeing a jumble of colourful shops and eating establishments, a horde of meandering people, and hearing nothing but the overwhelming hubbub of humanity.

The driver took a while approaching the site, as the roads were busy. Kerry had expected it. Such an odd, rare vision brought out everyone from the looky-loos to the actually interested. The driver pulled up, pointed, and let her out.

Kerry climbed out into the heat. A stiff, warm breeze caressed her face. She smelled salt and vegetation and maybe a whiff of decay. Her mouth had gone dry. The beach stood to her right, a row of houses across a narrow road to her left.

But it was the incredible black leviathan just

ahead at the edge of the sea that took all her breath away.

Some time during the night a passing typhoon had dredged up a galleon, an intact sunken ship, and thrust it onto the beach. Waves lapped at its stern. Kerry saw crustaceans along its side, as if it had been laid on the ocean bed that way. She saw its battered masts and even some rags for sails, and the high, proud thrust of its prow. It stood like a living picture of days gone by, prominent and majestic and glaringly conspicuous.

Kerry just looked at it for a moment. The sight of it just sitting there stirred her. It was the archaeologist inside, the fact that here was a new mystery waiting to be explored. Again she checked the chunky watch on her wrist – half past four – and blinked for a moment.

The watch had been her father's. It didn't suit her – didn't look right on her slender wrist – but he had loved it, and she never took it off. It was a constant memory, and one she needed. Now, she took a deep breath and started for the galleon, walking along the pavement as far as she could before turning right onto the beach, and approaching a gaggle of official looking people.

Kerry introduced herself. There were a lot of blank faces, but then a dark-haired woman wearing white sunglasses scrunched up her face and nodded.

'Yes, I remember,' she said. 'Kerry Roberts from New York, right?' She spoke with an American accent.

'Yeah, that's me,' Kerry said, pleased to find an ally. 'What have you got for me so far?'

'Well, we only just got started,' the woman said. 'But there are a few preliminary findings.' She held out a hand. 'Danielle Reid.'

Kerry blushed a little. 'Sorry. When I arrive at a site, my focus just narrows down.'

'It's no problem,' Danielle shook and then gestured at the ship. 'First, have you seen the damn name?'

Kerry squinted upwards towards the nameplate, her eyesight not brilliant through years of squinting at small artefacts. 'Are you kidding? What kind of name is that for a ship?'

'Hellhound,' Danielle all but whispered. 'I've never heard anything like it.'

For some reason, the speaking of the name made Kerry shudder. 'What else do you have?' she asked quickly to hide her discomfort.

'Don't worry. I felt the same way. And it doesn't get any better. The ship is being guarded day and night, right? Well, late last night, the guards heard noises coming from it.'

'Noises?'

'Just that. In the dead of night, they say, things were moving. Shifting.'

'Are they trying to say it's haunted?'

'They didn't say anything. It's just in the report.'

Already, Kerry wasn't liking what she was hearing. 'Anything else?'

Danielle ran a hand through her dark hair. 'It creaks.'

'It creaks?'

'Yeah, when you least expect it. The damn thing lets out a sharp creak, as if it's trying to scare the shit out of you.'

'Well, it is a galleon made of wood. It's expected to creak.'

Danielle made a face as if to say *you'll see* and then moved on. 'It's nicely intact. Incredibly so. We're safe inside, moving around. The decks are firm, the masts wobbly but sound.'

'Have you made any headway as to origin?'

'Like I said, we just got started, and the damn name's thrown us. We're still checking, but it appears that there's never been a registered ship by the name of Hellhound.'

Kerry stared at her. 'You have to be kidding.' She looked at the sheer size of it. *Nothing?*

Danielle shrugged. 'Very strange, I agree. Another mystery regarding this thing.'

Kerry took an involuntary step back. The galleon seemed entirely too large to never have been heard of. She didn't understand how such a thing might happen. Someone, somewhere, had sailed this vast thing on the seas. And the name... it was odd.

'No strange noises in daylight?' She asked.

'Not so far. But, listen, there's more.'

Kerry wasn't sure she wanted to hear, but swallowed and bit her bottom lip. 'Go on.'

'We have three local archaeologists already aboard. They've been there all day, checking carefully around. Now, they've come across the usual stuff, but aren't cataloguing anything yet. They're using the first day for familiarisation.'

Kerry nodded. It was what she was doing. 'Go on.'

'Well, this sounds strange, I agree, but they've found some sculptures and engravings inside the ship that they don't want any part of. The very sight of them scared the archaeologists.'

Kerry made a face. 'Are they green?'

'No, these guys are seasoned pros. It's all very-'

'Odd. Yeah, I get it. Listen, Danielle, we're gonna get into all this deeply. I don't speculate. I only find and present the facts. One wrong assumption can destroy you in this field. That's why I'm careful, exacting, and understand you're only remembered for your mistakes.' She held up a hand. 'Not entirely true, I know, but it's how I look at it. I love my job. It's my whole world. But it can be ruthless if you're not careful.'

Danielle nodded, being in the same field. 'When do you want to get started?'

'How long do we have the light for?'

'Another hour. Maybe ninety minutes.'

'Are all the lights set up inside?'

'Afraid not. It's still ongoing, and we're being meticulous. Most of today was health and safety.'

'Annoying, but essential,' Kerry laughed. 'It's hard when you're champing at the bit and a H and S officer holds up his clipboard and points his pen at you.'

Both archaeologists laughed, sharing a private joke. Kerry decided she would use the time to peruse the outside of the ship and start properly on site in the morning. She said her thankyous to Danielle and drifted away, following the side of the ship towards the sea. It loomed large and dark above her, wooden sides jutting out. She saw oars and railings and, craning her neck, the sorry-looking masts that even now flapped forlornly in the wind. The galleon did indeed shudder softly to itself, but nothing like how Danielle had described it. Kerry wondered if some kind of shared fear was creeping in to her team. She had seen it happen before on various digs.

She walked as far as the waterline and then went around the prow, looking up at the proud outline. There was a carving up there, but it was too far away to make out. She stared at the odd name — *Hellhound* — and wondered why anyone would name their vessel in that way. Kerry wandered around the other side, her eyes constantly searching.

Darkness started creeping in around the edges. Kerry decided to call it a day and ordered a taxi back to the hotel. She said her goodbyes to Danielle and agreed to meet her the next morning. That's when she would start her investigation in earnest. She saw nothing through the windows on her way back, instead letting her mind tick. A highly interesting mystery lay before her, and it was only deepening. Of course, something like this could enhance her reputation, or harm it. She had always been a meticulous, thorough examiner and something this important only made her instincts sharper, more distinct. The information she had received so far was hazy, to say the least.

Noises? Creaking? Scary sculptures? It didn't sound professional at all.

Kerry would bring all that tomorrow. For now, she climbed out of her taxi, entered her hotel, and went straight to the restaurant area. She was famished. She sat with a steak and a glass of wine and chilled out, knowing tomorrow would bring a far harder day. But now she was tired, jet-lagged, and needed rest.

When she headed up to bed, the things on her mind were the strange name of the ship and the fact that it had never been registered. Darkness had fallen outside. Night had set in. Were there noises in the dead of night? What was stirring? Did the Hellhound have incredible secrets to share?

Only time would tell.

CHAPTER THREE

Kerry's next few days passed as quickly and as full of action as the typhoon that had thrown the ship up. But slowly and surely, she began to build up some context of what the Hellhound was all about.

There were still noises in the darkness, still violent creaking and strange echoing trumpet sounds which no one seemed able to explain. You became used to it, or at least Kerry did, barely noticing it after the first day. She climbed on board, introduced herself to all the other members of the team, and set about her business. On the quiet, she was in charge, but it wasn't a position she would enforce. There were too many locals and other nationalities aboard, too much potential for loggerheads. Kerry preferred her operations to run smoothly, and if that meant a lot of diplomacy, then so be it.

Days passed. Kerry found herself in what might have been the captain's cabin, unrolling and reading many old scrolls. Her knowledge of the ship and its sailors was expanding. The builders of the great galleon had a name for themselves – the Cerberim. Or Cerbs for short. They spoke about themselves profusely in the scrolls.

As she worked, Kerry had a chance to check out

the so called 'scary' carvings. On first look, they made her shiver, sent an arrow of fear up her spine. Some depicted grotesque faces, stretched impossibly, screaming and dying. Others showed what could only be called demons, with outsize teeth and snarling mouths and elongated eyes. Still more were sculptures of people being sacrificed in horrible ways. There was something utterly obscene and evil about them.

It put the whole operation on edge. These carvings were everywhere – throughout the inside of the ship. Kerry managed to ignore them, but not everyone did. She saw eyes attracted to them everywhere she went, people looking uneasy, and she sought to shore them up, to bolster their confidence with a joke and a smile. She needed these people to be at their best, not running scared.

Through reading the scrolls, day after day, she learned more about the Cerberim. They were an ancient people or large tribe that had existed on an island chain somewhere, and they were highly feared. They were powerful, raiding other places by boat, often bringing back vast treasures with them. It seemed they worshiped dark forces – they had some evil gods and pacified them in the only way they knew how – with violent human and animal sacrifice. The Cerberim were a malevolent people, following vile gods and committing terrible deeds. In the scrolls, they rejoiced about their deeds, but it only made the reading harder and more dreadful.

Kerry read with horrible fascination. She positioned herself close to the captain's ruined desk and read intensively, learning everything she could.

It was a hard few days, but she found out even more about the unknown people.

This ship – the Hellhound – had been carrying settlers trying to expand the territory of the Cerberim. They had been given wealth and history and a vessel, the means to establish another outpost, and had gone searching for new lands where they could settle. So the Hellhound was a search vessel, a settlers' boat. It must have gone down with all hands. Kerry wondered if maybe a colossal typhoon or an earthquake destroyed the Cerberim themselves, because for some reason they had fallen out of history. Another alternative was that they had been so evil, so reviled, that scholars and historians deliberately *wiped* them out of all history.

She read on, finding more scrolls in sealed iron chests, drawn into the deeds of the Cerberim. She lost track of time, often staying until after dark. One night, she heard the noises start up and tracked them belowdecks to the area where a couple of small jail cells stood. The cells were shabby, the iron bars pitted and eroded from their time submersed, but Kerry felt a coldness hanging around. Singapore itself and the rest of the ship was too hot – the cells were cool and creepy. Feeling unsettled, she quickly got out of there.

More history told of more voyages and land raids and battles. The Cerberim grew in number and in daring, and quickly amassed great wealth. They were unmatched on the seas, dreaded by the various islands dotted around. Kerry read many stories of conquest, of invasion, and subsequent slaughter. But they had also been boatbuilders, navigators, historians. They weren't just a mindless, destructive race – there were some clever people living among them. Most likely, leading them and sending them into battle. All it needed was one mad bastard with a thirst for power, she reflected, and then that person rises to the top.

Days passed and Danielle helped her profusely. The other archaeologists kept their distance, documenting their own things, but they came together occasionally to match notes, ensuring they were going about it all in the correct manner. Kerry knew what she wanted, and despite the seclusion, the indifference of her companions, their reluctance to study the carvings, the operation seemed to be coming along just fine.

As she worked, though, Kerry detected an undercurrent of openness in her colleagues. She started to distrust them. They talked openly of their finds and their theories, and not just among themselves. She wondered if some of them might be passing along information to outsiders, maybe even being paid for it. It was their unguarded, lackadaisical manner, the fact that they discussed the galleon on their way out on an evening and then met with groups of people outside, still talking. Kerry thought about it all and then shrugged it away. She would go with the flow.

The galleon's presence was unmistakable, and people were naturally curious. It drew everyone, and there would always be someone trying to make a profit from something like this. It wasn't Kerry's job to police them.

For now, she would just do the job she loved, and

if that meant spending all day and all night in an old, reeking, rundown, and highly revered ship, then she would do just that.

CHAPTER FOUR

Matt Drake raised a bottle of beer and clinked with the others. They were sitting uncomfortably aboard a transport plane on their way back from Croatia, and they had just completed their first mission as part of the new agency.

'To Spear Solutions,' Drake said. 'May it long continue.'

The others echoed his words, all smiling. The name Spear Solutions had been suggested by Kinimaka, and it harked back to their days as Team Spear. Those were good, well-remembered days, and the entire team had been unanimous in their acceptance of the new name.

Alicia half emptied her bottle and then sighed. 'I deserved that. I think Mai and I worked rather well together in that last fight.' She sounded surprised.

Drake was shocked too. 'When you two attacked those four blokes together, coming in from two sides, it was perfection. It looked synchronised. I guess it's because we've been working together for so long.'

'And Hayden and I,' Kinimaka said. 'We rescued the good guy.'

They all took a quick glance at the outsider on the plane. Thomas Vance was a wealthy business executive who had been kidnapped by some lowlife Croatians. The team had got the job through a connection of Drake's old boss – Michael Crouch – and had jetted off to Croatia forthwith. After Patrick Sutherland – their friend and assistant director of the FBI – greased some wheels with the Croatian authorities, they had also been allowed to conduct their own operation in the city of Zagreb. Two days later, they had rescued Thomas Vance.

The op didn't go without its sticky moments. Dahl had tried to save the day by bursting in through a large glass window. He'd become caught on the rough shards and exposed to their enemies and had had to be saved by Mai and Kenzie. It wasn't his best moment, and Drake hadn't even started ribbing him about it yet. Those days would come, and they would be beautiful. The team had been up against twice their number, but had been victorious, not only rescuing Vance but taking down the entirety of the Croatian's operation, ruining it. They had destroyed the bad guys' infrastructure and taken a lot of them out with it. On the quiet, the local police had been extremely grateful.

Now, there was a celebration to be had. Their first mission was a resounding success and the man partying with them was living proof. He seemed to have taken quite a shine to Alicia, and the Englishwoman was egging him on.

She finished her drink and walked over to him now. 'Wanna dance?' she asked, as Mai shook her head.

'I don't dance,' the man said uncertainly.

'Neither do I, but it doesn't mean we can't bump and grind a little.'

Drake ignored her antics, confident in their relationship. He turned instead to Dahl. 'How're you doing, mate? Any cuts and bruises?'

The big Swede knew exactly what he was getting at. 'Piss off.'

'What's wrong? You *hung up* on something?'

'You'll find out if you keep on pushing it.'

Drake let it go for now. He had many more hours of fun ahead. He checked his watch. They were still a few hours out from Washington, DC, and their new office. It had been quite the change, becoming a legitimate working business. It had taken Hayden quite some time to make it happen. But, between her and Kinimaka, the hard logistical work had been done, and they had finally become a legal entity with ambitions and contacts and everything else they needed to make it work. Of course, they were still learning the ropes and would be for years, and they'd probably make a few mistakes along the way, but that was all part of the journey, wasn't it?

He leaned back. Alicia made her way to his side and tapped his shoulder.

'That guy won't dance with me,' she said a little drunkenly.

'Stop harassing him. He's a client.'

'But he's cute!'

'So am I. I'll give you what you need later.'

'Oh, promises, promises. Can we talk about it now?'

Drake smiled and shook his head. Alicia put her cheek on his shoulder. Their client looked decidedly confused.

'Don't worry,' Mai told him. 'She's a fruitcake at best.'

The rest of the flight passed mostly uneventfully. But just as they were about to begin their descent into DC, Drake's phone rang.

He checked the screen and answered. 'Aye up, Michael.'

His old boss, Michael Crouch, was on the other end of the line. 'How's it going?'

'Yeah, as expected. We rescued the businessman. He's here with us now.'

'You completed the op already?'

'This is the Ghost Squadron. We don't mess about, mate.'

'I thought you were Spear Solutions now?'

'Sure, that too. We go all ways.'

'Amen to that,' Alicia said quietly.

'How did it go? Any problems?'

Drake was tempted to mention the Dahl issue, but a knowing look from the Swede stopped him. He thought back to the last few days.

'All good,' he said. 'Cooperation from the cops was first class. We tracked the Croats to this warehouse in the industrial district and took an evening to scope them out, made sure the client was on site, and then hit them the next. Took their business apart, too. Made sure the boss men wouldn't live to corrupt another day with their presence. I think our reputation's intact.'

'Is the client in one piece?'

'Yeah, he's good. Alicia's been trying to cheer him up in her own special way.'

'Really? On the plane? And I thought you two were together now?'

'I don't mean like that,' Drake hurried the conversation on. 'We'll be looking for another mission come tomorrow.'

'And even before the money's in the bank. I'll keep my ear to the ground.'

Drake thanked him and hung up. It was largely

down to Crouch and a couple of other old contacts that they had started off on the front foot with the new agency. It was a good sign, and they needed the money. They had a lot of mouths to feed.

Drake's thoughts went to Cam and Shaw, who had sustained some bad injuries during the previous mission. They were still taking it easy, still recovering, mostly from home. They were still very much part of the team, but not active members yet. Of course, they wanted to be involved in the day-to-day business, but they weren't quite ready.

It was a content, happy team that touched down at Dulles airport and taxied their way to one of the side terminals. A team looking forward to the future. A team both surprised and grateful that they'd changed their objectives in such a relatively short timeframe. It was only a few months ago when they were working for a private security firm when the boss had been murdered.

Mai still dwelled on that. She had been very close to Connor Bryant, the owner of the firm. The Japanese woman was trying to move on and struggling. She had lost too many important people in her life.

They all had. Drake still remembered old, long gone friends as if they were still here today. Old colleagues too. They had known many people during their time together. The faces of those friends still burned the back of his retinas.

Spear Solutions was all about moving forward. It was fresh, and it was new, and it promised a lot of forward momentum. They could do different things with the new company, and they could forge new boundaries. More importantly, they could do it together. The future was bright.

Drake couldn't help but wonder what was coming around the corner. There was always a surprise or two. He just hoped it wouldn't be too big for them to handle.

CHAPTER FIVE

Javier lounged around his pool, shielded from the baking heat by a thick, deep blue parasol. To his left and right were women in bikinis and one-pieces, and guards wearing shoulder holsters to house their guns. Behind him were more guards, stationed near the doors, only these men carried sub-machine guns. Similar guards were posted throughout the house. Javier stared at the sparkling waters, listening to the waves lapping, watching the rising, diffused sun through the umbrella. The women were sprawled out, dozing or reading. A couple were eating and drinking. For now, Javier paid them no mind. He was thinking solely about business.

He was an arms dealer, a drug dealer. He dealt with the worst human scum of society. Or at least, his lieutenants did. Javier farmed most of the jobs off to them and oversaw it all, making sure everyone stayed in line. In Singapore, he was known as a kingpin, a high-up criminal practically above the law. He liked to think of himself that way. He looked up as a male servant brought him a silver tray bearing a coffee cup and a croissant. A good way to start the business day.

He sat down, ate, and drank. Through his mind

were flitting all his various operations, and the ones he'd need to bear in mind today. There was the deal with the Russians, the job on the stony ground where all the Croatians had vanished, the drug exchange in Amsterdam that involved his people and a bunch of enterprising Americans. He had no real reason to worry about any of them.

He made a call, sipping coffee. Made sure his second lieutenant was au fait with the Americans, and had enough back up. He needn't have worried. He made another call, came up with similar conclusions.

The morning was passing fast. One of the women – he paid for them to be at his beck and call – came over to ask if he needed anything, but he waved her away. Javier's mind was turning to smaller tasks, other things that might be happening in his city.

Javier had eyes and ears everywhere. He liked to think he was the most well-connected man in the city. There were contacts inside the police force, the judicial establishment, the banking system, the teaching organisation. He had men and women inside rival gangs, with influential speakers, in the orbit of social media influences. He had people where he didn't really need them, but Javier wasn't happy unless he had *all* the information. He could make better informed decisions that way.

More time passed. Eventually, Javier's thoughts came around to something strange that had happened during the typhoon. Nobody could fail to miss the enormous, mysterious ship that had come up out of the sea and deposited itself on the beach. It was a talking point for all the town. Even his guards were talking about it.

Javier looked up as one of his men came over to him, casting a shadow. 'Yes?'

'Hey boss, you remember that snitch, Julio? He ratted us out to the cops before we pulled the arms depot heist last month.'

Remember him? Javier still had nightmares about the near miss. 'I definitely do.'

'Some of the boys just caught him in Queenstown. Scooped the bastard up as he was crossing the road, right out of the blue.'

Javier's face broke out into a wide grin. 'They did? How fortunate.'

'Not for him,' the guard grinned back.

'Indeed. Have him brought to the arms warehouse tonight. I will make sure I'm there to watch.'

'Anything... special... boss?'

'Let's do machetes, cleavers and axes,' Javier said contentedly. 'We'll do an inch at a time. Make an example of the bastard.'

'Sounds good.' The guard turned and walked away.

Javier couldn't keep the smile off his face now. Today was turning into one of the best. He picked up his phone and dialled a number.

'Yes?' a voice answered quickly.

'Lee, is that you?'

'Oh, Hi. Yes, yes, Mr Javier, it is me.'

Lee was always deferential, not just to Javier, but to everyone. Javier liked that about the young man.

'Do you have anything to report?'

'Oh, yes Mr Javier, I do. There are four archaeologists here. *Four.* So it is all very serious. The galleon is worth a fortune. The scrolls found inside are invaluable, but to history. They speak of a lost tribe called the Cerberim, who were very bloodthirsty and vicious. They accumulated much treasure-'

'Is it aboard the ship?' Javier asked quickly.

'Unfortunately not, or it doesn't seem to be. There is one archaeologist here – an American woman – who takes it all very seriously and has been through the entire vessel already. She reads the scrolls and makes her notes and keeps her findings quiet. She won't speak unless she's reached a decision. The other archaeologists though – they speak a lot.'

Javier wasn't really into the politics of the mystery. The reason that the Hellhound had popped up on his radar was because of the potential treasure that may or not be inside, the ship's worth. He was always in the market to make more money.

'What do these archaeologists say? And remember, I'm only interested in the money side of things.'

'Yes, Mr Javier. The Cerberim were conquerors who worshipped evil gods and made human sacrifices. They subjugated many people, many races, using the sea to travel from shore to shore. They appear to have amassed a vast fortune. The only problem is, the scrolls do not state where their homeland is. At least, not yet. And it mentions the oppressed states, but not their exact whereabouts or people. I imagine the Cerberim didn't mind who they mastered and didn't care for identities.'

'So no clues as to this actual treasure they hoarded?'

'No, Mr Javier, but we are all still looking, and I have my ear to the ground always.'

'That's good. Keep me informed. If this treasure location surfaces, I want to be the first to know.'

'Of course, Mr Javier.'

It wasn't much, but it had been worth a five-minute phone call. Javier had interests in anything where money was involved, not just guns and drugs. He even had a side business in extortion and blackmail, but that was more of a personal hobby. He loved finding dirt on wealthy business executives and politicians, the latter in particular. There was nothing like making a politician squirm under your thick, heavy boot.

Javier leaned back. He liked the idea of chasing after the treasure of the Cerberim. It would prove a pleasurable distraction. But he had no illusions – the real money would be made with more material items. He had a business to concentrate on.

It was getting on for late afternoon now, and he'd had enough of the sun. He retreated into the air-conditioned house, enjoying the dimness compared to the outside. In here, it was pleasant, and the guards stood around with their guns, always reassuring.

Javier began to look forward to an evening filled with sharp metal blades and soft flesh and vengeance.

CHAPTER SIX

Kerry Roberts was into her second week investigating the Hellhound and its many scrolls. She'd discovered much about the Cerberim's history, about their proclivities and peculiar tastes, about their inclinations towards war. She'd learned about their gods and their idols. The strange carvings now made sense, and she sought to explain them to the other archaeologists, who still carried a measure of fear when they came face to face with one. It was the ones concerning human sacrifice that threw her, because there was no defending that.

Kerry worked all hours, often returning to the hotel after the restaurant was shut and having to beg something from room service. If that wasn't available, she was down to a biscuit snack, or a bit of fruit. Already, she'd lost weight. She was getting on fine with all her friends aboard the galleon, but often had to ask them to reduce the volume of information they were giving out. But, truth be told, there really wasn't anything all that juicy yet.

She was working her way through the scrolls diligently and meticulously. As she'd previously told Danielle, she didn't rush to conclusions and wouldn't make any unless she was sure. The less said, the better until the information was verified. Kerry wrote an entire book of notes, keeping everything close.

And she was down to her last few metal chests. She'd had kept an elaborate, threatening chest for last, wondering if it held some big secret. It was about two feet long by one foot wide and three high. It sported a wide-open screaming mouth on the top right where you would place a hand, and a massacre theme around the sides – dozens of people being slaughtered by marauding hordes. The chest was intimidating, and alarming, and something she didn't really want to lay her hands on.

But today was the day. She'd missed dinner last night, so made sure she had more than a full continental breakfast this morning before she went out. She arrived at the Hellhound almost wobbling because she'd eaten so much. The other archaeologists arrived about the same time and gave her a look of sympathy.

'Today's the day, huh?' One mumbled.

'I really *don't* envy you.' Another said.

'Call me if you need me,' Danielle said. 'I'll be there.'

'I'll be okay, thanks,' Kerry told them, and really believed it. It was just a chest, after all, an inanimate object that couldn't hurt you.

Before she ventured into the captain's cabin and tackled the final chest – Kerry wasn't about to open it late last night when midnight was striking – her thoughts ticked back to a discovery they'd made yesterday. Continuing to read the scrolls, they'd found that the Cerberim secreted their entire wealth in somewhere they called the Underworld. There were only a few references to the place, but Kerry had been exalted to find this new piece of information. The Underworld was clearly an actual place, and they'd quickly read on to find a reference to its location.

But there was nothing. Just a description of high caverns and spectacular caves and ice and snow and incredible wealth. It mentioned jewel filled niches and ledges and brought in mind for some reason one of the other archaeological sites she'd once visited known as the Gates of Hell. Kerry would never forget that site.

The rest of the scrolls mentioned the Underworld just half a dozen times, but they didn't reveal its location.

Now, Kerry clambered through the ship until she stood in the captain's cabin before the final chest. It sat ominously on a table, waiting for someone with the courage to come near it, to open it up.

Kerry walked forward. The ship creaked around her; the floorboards protesting. Through an open window, a gust of wind entered and whirled around the cabin. She could hear the rush of the waves on the beach, the shouts of people beyond the yellow cordon. Coming through the passageways, she could even hear her companions' voices as they catalogued elsewhere. They all sounded happy enough.

Kerry took a deep breath. She came to within a foot of the chest and let it out. Then she reached forward, grabbed the chest with two hands, tried not to close her eyes, and cracked it open.

The top came up with a shriek of protest that set her nerves on edge. Inside, there was darkness and a pale grey shadow. Kerry knew what it was before she reached in to pluck it out.

A single, well-filled scroll. It curled around the entire chest.

She reached in and unfurled it, laid it on the table, and used rocks for weights to keep the paper flat. Then she leaned over to read what she had found. As she did so, she heard a noise behind her and quickly whirled around. She blinked; her archaeologist companions were all standing there, offering support. She smiled and beckoned them over.

'Let's do this together,' she said.

Silence blanketed the room, and the only sounds were those odd creaks that seemed to fill the ship. By now, even the most fretful archaeologist had managed to put them to the back of their minds, so the group barely noticed.

Kerry read through the text quickly, her eyes widening. Then she read slower and slower, taking it all in. Her heart started beating faster and sweat formed on her brow. This was the real deal.

'Are you reading this?' Danielle said.

There was a hushed reverence. Kerry had never heard a bunch of archaeologists stay absolutely quiet for so long. She used the time advantageously, taking in every ounce of information from what was clearly a very special scroll.

'What we have here is the motherlode,' a man nicknamed Kip said. 'And we saved it for last. I think that's a kind of vindication, don't you?'

Kerry ignored the chatter that now started up. She was still trying to take in the scroll's information and what it might mean. After a long time, she was ready to talk.

'It's a key find,' she said softly. 'It explains the nature of this ship, and the people on it. It explains what they were doing. Where they were going. And beyond that... it gives us a clue as to the whereabouts of the Underworld.'

The others were nodding excitedly. Danielle pointed at the scroll. 'The travellers were settlers, embarking on a long voyage to find new homes, new territories for the Cerberim to live in. They were pioneers, I guess, seeking new lands. Uninhabited lands where the Cerberim could take over and thrive. They have my respect for wanting to embark on a mission like that.'

'They were,' Kerry said. 'I wonder how far they got. Maybe we'll never know.'

'Judging by the perfect state of the galleon even though it's been at the bottom of the ocean for hundreds of years, I'd say not far,' one woman said, with a hint of a smile in her voice.

Kerry wouldn't speculate. It wasn't her style. She dealt in cold, hard facts. And the only facts here were the ones written in front of her. 'It seems the Cerberim chose to put down the location of the Underworld for future generations, and in case the settlers needed part of the wealth to survive,' she said.

'But they haven't revealed the location,' Kip said. 'Just a clue that leads towards it.'

'Their thinking is that the settlers probably know the answer to that clue and could easily find their way. Anyone else – an outsider...' Kerry spread her hands. 'Would struggle.'

'Have you read the bit where it says the

Underworld is *guarded?*' Danielle said in a hushed voice. 'What the hell does that mean?'

Kerry wouldn't hypothesise, but that didn't stop the others.

'Guards,' someone said. 'People with swords and arrows.'

'An army,' Kip said. 'Watching the entrance.'

'Traps,' Danielle ventured. 'It's the most productive way. You wouldn't leave people to guard it. They'd need food, drink, living accommodation, a structure. You wouldn't leave an army. Too costly. So, the next best thing is to leave behind a bunch of traps.'

Kerry pursed her lips. She read the entire scroll again as they chatted, taking it all in. 'Let's deal with the facts before us,' she said. 'And the real fact is... that clue.'

The others crowded around, re-reading it themselves. Kerry was aware there wasn't much space between them.

'*To the home of the Cerberim, find the three criss-crossing peaks and go east through the forest, passing the heart lake, out of the trees and look in the mountains ahead for the crescent cave. And there, guarded, you will find the chest.*'

'And that's not all,' Danielle said. 'Because you need a starting place.'

Kip took over. '*From the southern tip of Malay Land, travel thirty leagues to the diamond bay where the Towering Peak overlooks the ocean and marks the land of the Cerberim.*'

Kerry struggled to take it all in. Right here, in front of her, was an incredible quest, a spectacular expedition. It offered excitement and thrills, but it also offered danger. It wasn't something you could embark on lightly. But it was everything she lived for. The galleon had indeed yielded up a trove of wonders.

'What's the next step here?' someone said. 'What do we do next?'

To Kerry, the answer was as clear as the mysterious scroll in front of her eyes, as obvious as gold glittering at the bottom of a stream.

'We find the Underworld,' she said. 'We go out into the world, and we find it.'

'And the danger? The potential traps?' Danielle asked.

'We get help from someone who's done it before.'

'Oh, and I suppose you know someone just like that,' Kip said.

'As a matter of fact... I do.'

CHAPTER SEVEN

Matt Drake entered his relatively new office by pushing through a door off the street and then climbing a narrow set of stairs. At the top was a wide corridor with several different offices, all with their names printed on the obscure glass window above the doors. He walked past two before seeing Spear Solutions, and then entered.

Inside, it was a double space. There was a desk directly to the right where their secretary worked. A larger desk opposite was where one of them sometimes sat to deal with the humdrum of business work. The wall to the left of it was full of information and post-it notes, maps, and diagrams. It was where they planned to work out their missions beforehand. To the right of the large desk was a comfortable seating area where the team could sprawl out and a temporary plastic table which had come with the room. The walls were lined with largely unused filing cabinets.

Drake turned to their secretary, a tousle haired lady named Sabrina. She was a thin, no-nonsense woman who always appeared to be doing something important. Drake saw her as practical and efficient. She handled the day-to-day business with ease.

Sabrina wore long skirts and glasses and always had her hair scraped back, her lipstick full red, and her hands and wrists devoid of any jewellery. Drake knew she was married, but he'd never seen her wearing a ring.

'Morning,' she said brusquely now, tidying a file away.

'Morning. Am I the first?'

'So it would seem.'

It was their first morning back since the mission to Croatia. Drake had dragged himself out of bed so that he could make it at the time they all agreed should be the start of their day – 9 a.m. Not a tough hour to be on time, he thought.

He walked over to the coffeepot and poured himself a mug. It was black and hot and steamy, just as he liked it.

'Any news?' he asked as he sat down in one of the seats, mug in hand.

'You've been gone four days,' Sabrina said. 'I've dealt with two phone calls, two emails, and a load of spam. I've dusted, straightened the post-it notes, printed out a couple more maps. Oh, and I've restocked the fridge. Your Swedish friend enjoys his smoothies, I must say.'

Drake nodded, impressed. 'And of those two telephone calls, and two emails… anything interesting?'

Sabrina sat down. 'The first was an insurance company wondering if we were properly covered. The other was an automated call from Jeff Bezos explaining that I owed Amazon $254 and that if I pressed three, he would let me pay. Both emails were from car dealerships wondering if we wanted to hire a Cadillac and a Chevrolet, respectively. I kept them, just in case.' She smiled.

Drake blinked. 'Wow, you've been busy.'

At that moment, the door opened. Dahl walked in, looking as if he'd run the last mile. Drake made a point of checking the time. 'Took the time to wash your hair this morning, did you?'

'I don't have a tiny body like you, so I take longer,' the Swede replied, and then nodded at Sabrina. 'I'm not the only one who's late.'

One by one, the others began to appear. By nine thirty, the complete team had assembled, even Alicia, who Drake had left in bed this morning suffering from a migraine. She wore dark glasses and kept her head low and stayed off the caffeine.

'We'll get better,' Hayden said after making her appearance with Kinimaka. 'We're not used to this office work thing.'

None of them were, Drake knew. He had struggled to make it on time. And if they were sitting around in the office, they weren't making any money. He leaned back and sipped his coffee, watching the others.

'I don't enjoy waiting for phone calls,' Mai said.

At that exact moment, the phone rang. Mai's eyebrows shot up, as did Drake's. They all watched Sabrina answer the call.

'Spear Solutions,' she said, and then listened intently. After a few seconds, she turned to Drake. 'It's Cam. He wants to speak to someone.'

'Why him?' Dahl complained, nodding at Drake.

'He was here first, so he's in charge today.'

'I prefer it when you're in charge,' Dahl told Sabrina.

'Steady on,' Alicia said.

Drake grinned at Dahl and walked over to take the call on the large desk. Sabrina put Cam through.

'Hey, mate,' he said. 'How are you both feeling?'

'We thought we'd check on you after the mission. Did it go okay? Was it a success?'

'Everything went well,' Drake said. 'We rescued the client, sunk the bad guys in a pile of crap, earned some money. All in all, a good few days.'

'Great to hear,' Cam sounded strained. 'That's a good start.'

'How are you and Shaw, mate?'

Cam sighed. 'Not so well,' he said. 'We were gonna try to make it in today. Welcome you back. But the aches and pains are just too much. Shaw can barely move and I'm on those high-strength painkillers. I'm seeing double.'

The couple had been captured and tortured during the team's last mission involving a criminal figure called the Dark Tsar. It would be some time before they were properly back on their feet.

'Sorry to hear that,' Drake said. 'You take it easy, both of you. We'll look after the business.'

Cam thanked him and hung up. Drake turned to the others. 'There must be some admin to do,' he said haltingly. 'Something to tie the last mission up.'

'I've done all that,' Sabrina said. 'And sent off the invoice just this morning.'

'Oh,' Drake said, and looked at the others. 'So what the hell are we supposed to do?'

They all looked blank. Kenzie found fruit in the

fridge and started munching it. 'Hone our skills?' she suggested. 'Gun range? Fighting gym? Nunchuck dojo?'

'We've marketed ourselves well,' Dahl said, and Kinimaka nodded. 'We're an elite "fix-it" squad. That's the brief. We'll go anywhere and solve any problem, military based or similar. The assistant director of the FBI has our interests at heart, as do Michael Crouch and several other good contacts. We're still in touch with Glacier, and they should be able to give us a few jobs. Nobody said starting the business up would be easy.'

Drake knew the big Swede was right. He looked up as Sabrina made a noise.

'This is interesting,' she said. 'A Bona fide enquiry. A firm from Missouri wants to hire a group of bodyguards for a few of their employees who are visiting Africa in three weeks' time. They're checking our interest.'

'Three weeks?' Kenzie said with a sigh. 'Feels like a lifetime.'

'And what do we do if a job appears in the meantime with an indeterminate end date?' Kinimaka put in. 'Do we turn it down?'

'We always said we may have to split up,' Drake said with a shrug. 'I guess that's just what we do. How many bodyguards do they need?'

Sabrina read the email again. 'Doesn't say. Doesn't say how many employees are travelling either.'

'Let's sound interested and work out a bunch of questions,' Hayden said. 'We can go from there.'

Sabrina took out a sheet of paper and started a

list. The team chimed in as they thought of queries. It passed a good while, and then they all sat back, feeling they had completed some proper work as Sabrina typed the response.

Drake checked his watch. It was a little after ten-thirty. He hadn't had breakfast – as he'd been in a hurry – and was hungry. He wondered where the local sandwich shop might be, the best coffee place. Maybe they should enquire with the other offices. He was about to suggest they do just that when the phone rang again.

The team stared at it as if it was a bomb.

'Shit,' Alicia said. 'That's twice.'

Sabrina, also looking surprised, answered on the third ring. 'Spear Solutions.'

They listened as she listened. After a minute, she turned to Drake. 'I think you should take this.'

The Yorkshireman, leader for the day because he'd got there first, stood up and walked forward. He put the phone to his ear.

'Hello? This is Matt Drake.'

'Ah, yes, I remember you,' a female American - accented voice said. 'You probably won't remember me. My name's Kerry Roberts. We met at the Gates of Hell.'

Drake frowned and tried to remember the name. He certainly remembered the Gates of Hell. It had been one of their earlier missions.

'I'm sorry,' he said. 'I don't recall the name. What were you involved with?'

'I investigated the tombs and the traps, but that doesn't matter now. It's you I want. Your team. I'm told you can be hired these days?'

'Yes, how do you know that?' It was always important to know where your recommendations came from.

'Archaeological circles. You discovered a lot of important, ancient artefacts back in the day. The tombs of the gods. The bones of Odin. And more... the swords of Babylon. You were renowned. The archaeological world has kept tabs on you and when you popped up with a new investigative agency, they took notice.'

'I'd hardly say we're investigative,' Drake told her hastily, then looked at Hayden and Kinimaka, who had once worked for the CIA, Kenzie who had worked for the Mossad, and Mai, who had worked for the Japanese police force. 'But we could be.'

'I'd need you immediately to undertake an expedition. I'm in Singapore and you may have heard that an ancient galleon has recently been washed ashore. The galleon has yielded up some important clues as to the location of a great treasure. I've decided to go after it, and I want you on hand in case there are any... dangers.'

It was a lot to take in. Drake listened intently and then popped the speakerphone on. He asked her to repeat herself for the benefit of the others and then sat down. The team stared at one another.

'It's different,' Dahl said.

'It's new, and it's a job,' Mai said. 'And it's what we do.'

'Why do you expect danger?' Kinimaka asked.

'There may be others chasing the same thing,' Kerry said. 'A fair few people know of the clue and they're not known for keeping it quiet. It's a large team here. And there have been previous leaks. Also, the clue we've found states that the location may be guarded.'

'Does it say how?' Mai asked.

'I'm afraid not.'

'Of course not,' Drake said. 'That'd be too easy. You say you're in Singapore and you need us immediately?'

'Yes. Can you make it?'

'Drop us the address,' Drake said after seeing unanimous nods among his team. 'We'll be there as soon as the plane journey allows us.'

He stood up and grinned. 'A new mission,' he said. 'And it sounds juicy.'

'I'm so ready for this,' Hayden said.

'Grab as much gear as we'll be able to take,' Drake said. 'Including comms. This is a professional outfit now. Get packed. Sabrina, make the plane reservations. Everyone… we're on the first flight out.'

CHAPTER EIGHT

Drake looked out of the window as the plane circled the airport and prepared to land them in southeast Asia. It had been a pleasant flight with little turbulence, which suited him down to the ground. In past years, because of his time flying constantly with the SAS, he hadn't given turbulence a second thought, but these last few years, it had started to unsettle him a little. Yes, it was odd, he knew, but people changed.

They cleared the airport with no hassle and took a taxi to their hotel. It was evening here, and there was little point seeking Kerry until the morning. So, they took a walk into the Singaporean night, found a nice restaurant, and sat down for an enjoyable meal. Jet lag was already kicking in, and they felt weary. The meal helped.

Drake and Alicia retired to their small room soon after. Not even waiting for a shower, they set their alarms and fell asleep in their clothes, bone tired. When he woke up the next day, Drake was all woolly headed and wondering where the hell he was. It took several minutes to come around.

Soon, they'd met up with the others for breakfast and had contacted Kerry. The archaeologist asked to meet them at the washed-up galleon, which sounded pretty fair to Drake, since that was why they were here. He ate a full breakfast, washed down with copious amounts of coffee and water, and then led the others outside to their waiting oversized taxi. They were driven through busy streets packed with cars and people, and then through a shabby neighbourhood at the end of which stood the beach. The taxi turned left and then took a while to reach its destination. Drake could see the galleon standing out on the beach from a long way off. It was a clear landmark.

The taxi pulled up at the side of the road and let them out. Drake led the march across the sand to the side of the huge galleon that blotted out the sun. Drake shielded his eyes as he stared up at it, smelling the timber and the rot, the salt of the sea. He heard the chatter of those onboard; the waves lapping at the shore; the cars humming along the distant street. He reached out to touch the side of the ship, feeling the rough, hard wood against the tips of his fingers.

'You're Matt Drake,' a female voice said.

He turned. 'And I'm guessing you're Kerry Roberts,' he said to the woman standing close to them. He reached out a hand. 'Good to meet you.'

They made their introductions, and then Kerry led them inside the ship. Drake took it steadily, seeing the narrow wooden walkways, small cabins, and compact kitchen area. The roof above his head was dark timber, the floorboards loose and creaking. He thought that some of them hadn't dried out yet because they were so dark, but knew that was unlikely. The heat in this part of southeast Asia was intense at the moment.

Kerry took them to the captain's cabin. There was a low table in the middle with a weighted-down scroll sitting on it. The team took a moment to position themselves around the room. There wasn't a great deal of space.

'I thought I'd start off by showing you the special scroll,' Kerry said. 'And then I'll explain what it all means.'

Drake saw a few people hovering outside the door. He leaned close to Kerry. 'Do you trust your people?' he whispered.

She looked from him to the door. She shook her head. 'No,' she breathed back. 'They all talk. It's impossible to keep a secret here.'

'Good to know,' Drake said. 'Go on.'

'All right, well, this is the work of a people called the Cerberim. They were war mongers and worshipped dark gods, prone to human sacrifice. They ravaged the shores, attacked people and stole their wealth, hid it away in something they called the Underworld. When some pioneers started out on this ship – called the Hellhound – the Cerberim sent with them a clue as to the whereabouts of the Underworld in case they ever needed it.'

'A kind of "if you run out of money, go to this ATM" kind of thing,' Alicia said.

'That's it. The Cerberim wanted to look after their settlers as much as they could. This was the final scroll we unearthed. And the most telling.'

'So we're essentially chasing after the plundered wealth of a nation of born killers,' Dahl said. 'Looking for their blood money.'

'The Cerberim were an evil race,' Kerry affirmed.

'I've never heard of them,' Mai said.

'Nobody has that I know, either. We think they were relatively short-lived and capitulated to some natural disaster. Something that ended their entire existence. Maybe a tsunami, an earthquake or a super typhoon. That's the only explanation that makes sense. I've known tribes and even a whole people disappear that way before.'

'Look at Atlantis,' Alicia said.

'I know it was recently found,' Kerry said. 'But the Cerberim are hardly in the same league. Atlantis was huge.'

'Okay, so they're an unknown race,' Drake said. 'They were bloodthirsty, conquery, and loved a nasty god or two. They secreted all their stolen wealth in something they called the Underworld, and now you have a chance to find it.'

'In a nutshell, that's it,' Kerry said. 'The expedition will comprise quite a few people, so we need a team like you to be our guards.'

'At your service,' Drake said. 'We can do that.'

'The thing to remember,' Hayden said. 'Is that – if they find out – other factors will want a piece of this. To coin a metaphor – if this ship's as leaky as you say it is, then we're gonna have company at some point.'

Kerry nodded. 'See here,' she said, pointing at the scroll. 'This is the key passage: *To the home of the Cerberim, find the three criss-crossing peaks and go east through the forest, passing the heart lake, out of the trees and look in the mountains ahead for the crescent cave. And there, guarded, you will find the chest.*'

'It seems pretty straightforward,' Dahl said. 'But

where is the land of the Cerberim? Could it have been wiped out?'

'I certainly hope not,' Kerry said quickly, as if the thought hadn't occurred to her. 'We also have this translation: *From the southern tip of Malay Land, travel thirty leagues to the diamond bay where the Towering Peak overlooks the ocean and marks the land of the Cerberim.*'

'Malay Land?' Hayden questioned.

'In the olden days, it was called Malay Land. Today we call it Malaysia.'

'Not too far from here,' Drake said. 'So are we thinking the galleon didn't get very far?'

Kerry shrugged. 'Quite possibly. Any number of extreme events could have befallen it. Hopefully, we'll find the land of the Cerberim in Malaysia.'

'I noticed, as you said, that it reads *guarded*,' Drake said. 'Are there any clearer details?'

Kerry shook her head. 'We were thinking traps, that kind of thing. Do you remember the Gates of Hell?'

The team nodded as one. Drake still had nightmares about it and so, he knew, did Alicia. They had won the day, survived and been victorious, but the trauma of the journey had never left them.

'Yes,' Drake said shortly.

'I studied the traps after they'd been made safe. They were ingenious. Many mechanisms deteriorate over time, but these had survived because of their ingenious manufacture. I hope we don't find the same at the Underworld.'

'Or at this clue site,' Hayden added. 'Since that's exactly where we're headed.'

Kerry nodded, then rolled up the scroll and stored it safely in a metal tube. She indicated the walls.

'Out there,' she said. 'Most of the logistics have been organised already. There's a sizeable party going, so we have to think about sleeping arrangements, food, drink, and more. But it's doable, and a couple of us have been involved in something like it before.'

'Are you ready to leave?' Drake asked expectantly.

'Tomorrow,' Kerry said. 'We'll go tomorrow.'

CHAPTER NINE

'I don't do ships,' Alicia said unhappily.
'It's not a ship,' Drake said.
'You don't do anything without complaining about it,' Mai retorted.
'Oh, I wouldn't say that. Ask Drakey.'
'Well...' Drake said playfully before getting an angry look and getting back to work. He was currently helping loading food on board their large boat, as were all the other except Alicia, who seemed to prefer staring hard over the rolling waters and worrying. Drake got on with his task.

The team was on board. Besides Kerry, there was Danielle and another archaeologist named James. They also had five helpers or assistants, all of who liked to be aware of what was going on. And Drake couldn't really blame them. They were sailing into the unknown here.

A blistering sun blasted down from above, and there wasn't even a white cloud in the sky. The waters glistened, rolling gently, lapping at the dock, spreading out into infinity. The sea breeze was welcome and the noise on the docks was fierce. Drake had to jostle his way to and from their pile of goods every time, and they had to leave Dahl to watch over it just in case any chancer decided to run away with a box of pasta.

Soon, though, their rented boat was fully stocked and ready to go. They had also hired a captain who would sail them to their destination through the, hopefully, calm seas. It was Kerry's job to pass on their destination which, in the form of a vague few sentences, probably wouldn't endear her to the older man. Still, if he'd been sailing for a while, maybe he would even know their destination. Drake made sure he stayed close to Kerry.

The captain was standing with his back against one of the railings, watching the activity along the dock.

'Are you ready go?' he asked in halting English as she approached.

'Almost,' she said. 'We'll be there soon, I'm sure. Can I read you out our destination?'

The old man nodded, looking mildly surprised.

Kerry removed a slip of paper from the back pocket of her jeans. *From the southern tip of Malay Land, travel thirty leagues to the diamond bay where the Towering Peak overlooks the ocean and marks the land of the Cerberim.*

The captain frowned. 'Southern tip? Thirty leagues? Diamond Bay? Towering peak?' He shrugged. 'I can do that?'

'Does it ring a bell?' Drake asked.

The old man looked confused.

'I mean – do you recognise it? The description?'

A shake of the head and another shrug. The man pulled a chocolate bar out of his pocket and started munching. 'Tell when ready,' he said and turned away.

Kerry nodded. Drake turned to see Kinimaka carrying the last of the boxes on board. Alicia frowned at him and shook her head. He shrugged. She'd been alright the last time she'd been on a boat. Maybe it was an age thing... not that he'd ever voice that thought out loud. Or maybe – maybe Mai was right, and she just liked to complain. He smiled to himself, thinking he was venturing into dangerous territory.

Soon, the boat was ready to sail. The captain went into his cabin, still eating his chocolate bar, and fired up the engines. Drake heard a chug and clatter of mechanics and then a thick bellow of diesel smoke belched from the back, momentarily blotting out the sky. He winced. That didn't bode well.

He took a glance at the horizon. The waters were mercifully calm, gently rolling as far as he could see. The light bouncing off them hurt his eyes, so he turned away, wondering how the older man did it. But then, he'd been doing it for a lifetime.

The boat got underway, pulling free of the dock and turning. Drake guessed thirty leagues to their destination wasn't that far, but then he'd also been told by Kerry that Malaysia had 535 unnamed islands and the majority of them were never travelled to. The captain had his work cut out.

The captain turned their prow in the right direction, leaving the bustling dock and its glittering city behind. Drake didn't look back. His team was gathered near the doorway to the lower decks.

'Aye up,' he said, coming over to them. 'You ready for this?'

'Our second job as an agency takes me back a bit

to the stuff we used to do,' Hayden said. 'It's a pleasant change.'

'I'd feel better if we were armed,' Alicia grumbled.

'Agencies like ours can't take weapons on international flights,' Drake said. 'Not yet, at least.'

'There are exceptions,' Hayden said. 'But not this.'

Their words didn't improve Alicia's mood.

Mai stood close to the rail, holding on with both hands and gazing at the sea. 'Feels like an adventure,' she said. 'And we're getting paid this time.'

'That does kinda improve things,' Dahl said. 'We're getting paid for doing something we love.'

The Swede grinned as a warm gust of wind blew over them, bringing with it a spray of salty sea. Drake turned more to the matter at hand.

'What do you think of our quest?'

Kenzie was leaning against the closed door. 'I like it. Looking for this underworld, the land of the Cerberim. We could become famous.'

'We already are famous,' Kinimaka said drily. 'In certain circles.'

Drake winced a little at that. Not all those circles were agreeable. 'It's what we find at the end of the journey,' he said. 'And where it takes us.'

'Life,' Mai said. 'Is the same.'

Alicia snorted and turned away. Drake wondered what was actually wrong with the Englishwoman. She seemed out of sorts lately. He knew she's been worried about Cam, but Cam was fine now. He would make a full recovery, same as Shaw. Maybe Alicia wasn't enjoying their new venture. Maybe he should talk to her about it when they were alone.

Which wouldn't be for a while. They were together

as a team now until the end of this. Drake was thankful for that. He wasn't looking forward to the jobs where they would have to split up. He knew they were one of the best in the business, but he thought that was because they all worked well for each other, worked well as a team, possessed all the right moving parts. Testing that theory by splitting up wasn't necessarily a good thing.

Kerry exited the captain's cabin and came over to them. 'Well, he seems pretty confident he knows where he's going. At least he's converted the thirty leagues into nautical miles and knows what to look out for.'

'It's ninety nautical miles,' Kinimaka said with a smile. 'I could have told you that.'

Kerry looked at him in surprise. 'Okay, well, in ninety nautical miles we need to be looking port and starboard and trying to find those landmarks.'

Drake nodded. Hopefully, he thought, this whole thing wouldn't take too long and would be entirely non stressful. It had started out perfectly. On the whole, there wasn't an awful lot to go wrong.

CHAPTER TEN

The boat wasn't fast. Drake had been expecting to take a few hours to reach their destination, but not in the region of twelve. It was actually longer than that as night dropped and they were forced to drop anchor and wait for the morning light. They couldn't find landmarks in the dark.

With nothing much to do and not enough beds to sleep in, the entire team crowded into their cabin and ate food from cans. Luckily, there was enough whiskey to go around and soon the lack of space didn't matter as much. Drake found Alicia sitting on his lap was most enjoyable, but balked when she moved and Kinimaka tried to take her place. Most of them didn't sleep at all; the hours of darkness passing slowly, so it was with a sigh of relief that they saw the flash of a new dawn the next morning. Minutes later, the captain made an appearance, having spent the night in his own cabin.

'Eat, drink and get ready,' he said. 'Time to go.'

'How long?' Drake asked.

The captain shrugged. 'If we find quick, a few hours.'

Drake felt his spirits rise. He ate pastries and drank coffee in copious amounts and then ventured out on deck. The boat was already moving. To left and right the sea rolled, and there was the occasional land mass – an island. Some were so small they barely deserved the name, others were of a size that made him squint in earnest to make out their landmarks.

The morning started to pass. Still, the boat chugged on, the captain staying in his cabin and guiding them. The sun rose to a height where it shone brightly in their eyes, blocking out the view to the east quite successfully. It was lucky then that the captain's eyes were so good, as suddenly the boat started to slow.

He thrust his head out of the cabin. 'There,' he said and pointed. 'To east.'

Kerry was already craning her neck towards the new land mass. Drake stood at her side. The first thing he saw was the shape of the nearest bay.

A crescent.

He blinked, rubbed his eyes, and then looked for the towering peak. The sun was blinding but, through the bright haze, he made out a distant mountain. A large one. 'Could that be it?' he asked quietly.

Kerry stared hard, matching what she knew in her head to what she was looking at. Drake knew she didn't want to get this wrong.

'From here,' she said. 'It looks correct.'

'Well, that's definitely a diamond-shaped bay,' Mai said. 'That much is obvious. And look at the land. It's rocky, foresty, hilly. I can see fields too. And that's just from the shore. It might have been inhabited once.'

Kerry, listening, nodded her head. 'I agree. Let's anchor this thing and head inland.'

Drake was gazing intently at the island. It wouldn't do to get this wrong. But he guessed Kerry knew what she was doing, and if they followed the clues and found matching landmarks, then they would be on the right track. He helped load their backpacks with provisions and caving equipment, everything they'd brought from Singapore to help them on their journey. The only weapons they had were knives, but it didn't exactly look like they'd need them anytime soon.

The captain anchored the boat and invited them to climb down to the rowboat. It took two trips to ferry them all to shore, and now Drake found himself standing on a sandy shore, facing a long treeline and several mounds of rocks. From here, the high mountain was blocked out.

Kerry pulled out a sheaf of rolled up papers from her backpack. 'Right,' she said. 'Let's get our heads around this again.'

Drake listened intently to her words.

'To the home of the Cerberim, find the three crisscrossing peaks and go east through the forest, passing the heart lake, out of the trees and look in the mountains ahead for the crescent cave. And there, guarded, you will find the chest.'

Kinimaka shielded his eyes against the still bothersome sun. 'We're gonna have to climb a tree,' he said. 'To find the three criss-crossing peaks.'

Kerry didn't look impressed. Those assistants that spoke English raised their eyebrows and didn't exactly step forward. It was Mai who grinned and rubbed her hands together. 'I can do that,' she said. 'I'm good with trees.'

'Yeah, she can mount anything that looks like a pole,' Alicia muttered.

Mai gave her the finger and marched off towards a couple of tall trees. Within seconds, she was climbing through the branches and had soon reached a dangerous elevation, making Drake's breath catch in his throat. He wouldn't have liked to be that high, clinging to a tree limb.

Mai climbed higher and higher, probably forty feet off the ground. Now she was nearing the topmost, weaker branches and had to be extra careful. Drake's mouth had gone dry.

'Do you see anything?' Kerry shouted up.

Mai didn't answer. She was still climbing. A few more minutes passed. The sun blasted into Drake's eyes. Mai was standing on a precarious tree limb, looking out over the island and shielding her gaze. She stayed like that for a long time, scanning the horizons. After a while, she started to climb back down to the ground. Kerry waited with barely concealed impatience.

Mai jumped the last few feet and turned, a smile on her face. 'Well, that was fun,' she said. 'Took me back a bit.'

'What did you see?' Kerry asked immediately.

Mai pointed at the tree she'd climbed. 'From that marker,' she said. 'Six or seven degrees that way,' she waved. 'Stands an odd rock formation. It has three peaks, and yes, they do indeed cross on their way to the summit. We head east, at a direction of seven degrees from that tree.'

Kerry's face broke out into a big smile. Mai's words also confirmed they were on the right island. She shouted out their success to the crew. A cheer went up. Everyone was sweating under the sun right now, already looking the worse for wear, all shrugged into their backpacks and reaching for water. Drake wondered what they'd be like after a few hours hiking across the island.

Kerry mobilised them. They took out compasses and got their bearings, and started off through the trees. Mai was at the head of the pack, closely followed by Kenzie and then the assistants. The archaeologists made up the central core of their march, and then Drake and the rest of his team brought up the rear. Since Mai was leading, Drake knew he didn't have to check his own compass to ensure they were on the right track.

The forest thickened all around them to the point where it blocked out the sun. It became eerily quiet too, as if they were the only people on earth trekking to some unknown destination. The team, buoyant at first, soon fell into silence and followed Mai through the tree-infested undergrowth.

They marched for hours, heading through the occasional large clearing where wildflowers grew in abundance. The odd stream crossed their path, narrow enough to jump over and with low banks. Above, the sun dappled its way through the canopy, painting the forest floor bright in random patches, drawing the eye. Drake used the journey as an exercise session, stretching out.

After a while, Mai stopped, pausing for a break. She had chosen an open space to do so. There was sunlight and flowers and a nearby burbling brook. The entire team sank to their knees and broke out food and drink, taking their time to swallow their sustenance. They spoke in whispers, as if not wanting to shatter the calm that lay over the island. Kerry wondered aloud how many years it might have been since people stepped foot here.

'No ancient ruins yet,' Danielle said wistfully. 'I was hoping to run across something.'

'Well, you are an archaeologist,' Kerry said with a laugh. 'But it is a big island.'

'Plenty of places to look yet,' James, the other archaeologist, said.

After an hour's break, they were up again and following Mai through the forest. Drake hefted his pack, complete with camping gear if needed, and started off after her, maintaining his position in line. It seemed a waste of time setting a perimeter to watch out for trouble, but it was ingrained in him and he would never risk missing something. He assigned Dahl and Alicia to keep watch. Kerry, ahead, noticed his actions and frowned, but said nothing. She had brought them on as protection, and she let them do their job.

It took another half hour, but then the trees began to thin out. They crossed rolling hills for a while, now able to see the criss-crossing rock formation ahead occasionally, and to see Mai's navigation was spot on. They reached the top of a hill and paused, eyes raised at the sight below.

A heart-shaped lake.

Drake smiled a little. For him, this was the first real sign they were on the right island. The other landmarks could have been coincidences. But here, right now, was certain proof they had found the long-lost land of the Cerberim.

'The next part says the crescent cave should be in the mountains ahead,' Kerry said from memory. 'Those mountains, do you think?'

Drake followed her finger. Ahead, a small group of tall peaks thrust up to the sky. There were only about five of them, and it could hardly be called a range, but they were in the right place. And, more importantly, they were all that was on offer.

'Has to be,' he said, and then turned to Mai. 'Lead on.'

It was early afternoon by now, and the sun was high. It beat down on their heads as they walked through dried grasses and parched earth. Despite the heat, Drake didn't wish for any rainfall. He knew that when it rained in these parts, it could be quite spectacular. They toiled on; the mountains appearing never to come any nearer, until, finally, they were in the peaks' shadow.

Mai stayed on her course. Dahl and Alicia reported all was well and stuck to their assignments, trailing the team and looking out for trouble. Alicia mentioned she'd seen a tribe of cannibals back there, but they didn't seem interested in Dahl. Too chewy. They'd barely escaped with their lives.

Drake grinned and left them to it. At least they were entertaining themselves. Mai went on, leading the bunch of adventurers towards the mini mountains. As they walked, Kerry suddenly stopped and took a breath.

'Is that it?' she asked in an awed voice.

Mai had been concentrating on the terrain and the compass. Now she looked up. Drake stopped a few feet behind her. Ahead, in the sheer rock, stood a high, crescent-shaped hole. It was easily high and wide enough to take a person.

'That's it,' Drake said. 'Matches the directions perfectly.'

'It's only three p.m.,' Kerry said. 'We have plenty of time to explore, and no time to waste. Let's get to it.'

It was one of the assistants who held up a hand of warning. 'Remember,' he said. 'The use of the word "guarded" That could mean traps.'

His words filled Drake with foreboding.

'Alicia!' Mai shouted from the front. 'You go first!'

CHAPTER ELEVEN

Mai's joke didn't go down well, but Alicia and Dahl came in from the perimeter to discuss entering the cave. It was decided that the archaeologists themselves should go first, since they had the best knowledge and experience to locate any traps. None of the three were happy about it, but it was the best thing to do.

They geared up, taking some equipment out of their backpacks, including flashlights. It was a long procession of people that entered the cave, and the way forward was narrow enough to force them into single file. Drake found himself behind Kerry, who followed Danielle with James leading the way. Drake left Dahl and Alicia at the rear to watch their backs.

Total darkness soon enveloped them, and the torches were switched on. The cave had a musty smell, something ancient and dusty. The passage went straight for a while, and then started to slope down gradually, leading them deeper into the mountain. Staying narrow, the passage didn't deviate nor offer any offshoots, which was a blessing to the explorers. They'd hate to split up down here.

Drake tuned out the spooky keening noise that accompanied them. It had to be holes in the cave, letting in the wind and tuning it. The noise came often, sometimes quite loud and offputting. It sounded like someone mischievous trying to have a bit of fun.

The journey continued, sometimes heading sharply down and other times staying level. The passage rarely widened and even then just for a few feet, but it was worn smooth and no jutting rocks snagged their arms and legs, so it all went smoothly.

Drake was daydreaming a little, when ahead, the second in line, Danielle, tripped over a rock. The rock didn't fly away; it didn't roll over, but it did sink into the ground. Drake's mind got a grasp on how ominous that was at the same time as James let out a scream of fear.

From ahead, in the tunnel, a wall of timber shot straight towards them.

Drake grabbed hold of Kerry and threw her to the ground. Danielle stumbled to her knees. James, the closest, tried to leap out of the way. A row of spikes fronted the fast approaching timber wall.

It shuddered to halt just in front. James screamed again, falling to his knees. Behind him, Danielle stayed low, and Drake moved to cover Kerry, but the timber wall had come to a stop. It wasn't progressing further. In fact, just then it creaked its way back to reset. James was on his knees, cradling his left arm.

'It got me,' he said.

Drake ran forward, taking care not to step on the rock that triggered the trap. He knelt down next to James and leaned over to assess the damage.

Luckily, it wasn't too bad. A spike had grazed James, the object drawing blood that ran down his arm. There was a decent amount of it, though, and a wound that would take some healing. Drake turned to one of the assistants – the man who held all the first aid gear.

'Bandage, plasters and gel,' he said.

They carefully picked their way past the wooden trap before kneeling again to assist James. Drake bandaged him up tightly and gave him a smile. 'You're fine, mate. Just a scratch.'

'Hurts like a git,' the man said. 'Thought I was a goner.'

'It could have been worse,' Drake said. 'We have to be more careful from here on.'

He changed things around. The Ghost Squadron took point, being more used to looking out for dangers, though Drake didn't blame Danielle for stepping on the rock. It hadn't looked ominous in the least. But this team was there to protect, to lead the way, and that's exactly what they would do.

With the new formation, they carried on. Drake put himself up front with Kinimaka and Hayden just behind, and kept his eyes peeled for danger. Ten minutes further on, he saw another suspect rock and shouted it out. They passed the potential trap a few seconds later, just waiting to pounce. Drake took a deep breath. They had successfully passed the trap, but that didn't mean he'd catch the next one.

They continued on. Now, the passage headed upward for a while and then twisted to the right. They were certainly headed deep into the mountain. There was little chatter among the group and most had their heads down, slogging on. The team stopped for a break after a while, snacking and drinking, and spread out along the tunnel. If they had been hoping for a quick success story here, it wasn't going to happen.

Drake thought about that. It should have been obvious from the start that the Cerberim wouldn't leave their important clue near the entrance. They wouldn't want just anyone to stumble across it. It had been planted here for their people, the settlers who had departed on a vital task. They should have expected quite a slog to reach it.

He voiced his thoughts out loud.

Kerry nodded. 'I should have thought of that. The Cerberim aren't stupid people. They would have taken measures to protect their wealth even as they left clues as to its whereabouts. One might say that only the worthy will locate it, get to the final cave, or whatever it is. This trek won't be easy.'

Drake figured she was talking about the entire mission, not just this cave. He munched on a sandwich and listened to her talk of the Cerberim.

She warmed to her subject. 'Though warmongers, the Cerbs were an intelligent, complex people who valued their home as highly as they valued their gods. Home was everything to them and, to safeguard it, they decided to explore other lands in which to settle. They didn't want to outgrow this island, make it barren of produce, of foodstuffs and fresh water. That is why they chose to explore. They not only built seagoing vessels, but they built a great city – which is here somewhere – and monuments and statues. They were a convoluted people.'

'I think they were insane,' Alicia said. 'Murderers who sacrificed people they believed were their enemy.'

Drake sidled up close to her. 'Let's not upset the paying client,' he whispered in her left ear.

'That's one narrow-minded way of looking at it,' Kerry said. 'Yes, they did all those things, and they worshipped cruel gods, but they also cared for their homes, for their island, and for each other. They were a loyal people who stuck together and worked for each other. All that comes across so clearly in their writings.'

'No clue what happened to them?' Dahl asked.

'Whatever it was, it must have been very sudden and volatile,' Kerry said. 'As no record exists, not the slightest clue. As I said before, it could have been a rogue mega-typhoon, an earthquake, something like that. I fear we'll never find out.'

The group fell silent for a while until it was time to continue. After dragging themselves to their feet with a chorus of groans, they were ready to go. Drake started leading the way, but this time Dahl pushed in front of him, sharing the burden. The Swede pressed on carefully, always vigilant. Time passed as the group picked their way inexorably towards whatever fate awaited them.

'I wonder when the last person stepped foot in here,' one of the archaeologists asked.

Kerry coughed. 'Hundreds of years,' she said. 'The Cerberim were the last people to go this deep.'

Drake looked on at the ever descending tunnel. 'How deep does it go?' He wondered.

'To Hell,' Mai said. 'I think it goes to hell.'

Drake laughed without humour. 'The trouble is,' he said. 'You could be right.'

CHAPTER TWELVE

Down and down they went, the passage descending gradually. Dahl, in front, led the way slowly and cautiously. The group talked little as they progressed, just slogged on. The initial excitement of finding the cave wore off, and it was now a long, arduous trek. Drake thought that the only upshot was that it was all one way. There were no side passages.

After another long hike without encountering any traps, Dahl suddenly slowed. Drake sensed that the passage widened ahead, and soon the Swede was out of sight. He kept going, wondering what they were about to face.

He came out into a wide cavern. The first thing Drake really saw was the look on Dahl's face, which was alarming. He soon saw why.

Ahead, there was a wide gap, too wide to jump across. Drake saw the remnants of rock, just jagged edges on both sides of the gap as if maybe at one time a bridge had spanned it. If so, it was long gone.

'Could be an old trap,' Kerry said. 'The bridge may have just disintegrated with age.'

Drake looked left and right. 'There's only one way across,' he turned to the others. 'Climb.'

He walked to the edge of the gap, looked down. A

black hole fell away, the bottom maybe fifty feet deep, picked out by the flashlight. Drake looked behind him, up and around the cave. By now, everyone had crowded into the cavern, including their rearguard.

'No problems back there,' Alicia announced. 'What do we have here?'

Drake was already kneeling in front of a pair of packs. They had rock-climbing gear, simple things like rope and pitons. All they had to do was rig a way across and then use a harness to ferry everyone to the other side. Dahl was an excellent climber, as was Kenzie. Together, the two of them could easily rig something.

The Swede set off first, climbing up the rear rock face to the ceiling above, and then crawling his way across using the pitons. Soon, he came down the other side, fixing the rope in place. Kenzie came next, following the same route and fixing another rope. Soon, the duo had fixed two ropes in place and tested them with their own weight. The fixings were good.

Dahl smiled across the gap. 'Who's first?'

Drake shrugged and decided to take it. He fixed himself into a harness, attached it to the ropes and then started to swing himself across, hand over hand. The rope swayed and rocked, but it was strong and held perfectly in place. Drake had to slow down to stop the swinging, learning as he went. Soon, he too, was on the other side and sliding the harness back down the rope.

'Let's move it,' he said.

The operation went smoothly for everyone. They lost some valuable time when one of the aids got himself stuck in the centre of the gap, unable to pull himself further, but with a bit of help they managed to ferry him across, panting and sweating. The man swayed on the edge as he unhooked and would have fallen backwards if Kinimaka hadn't grabbed him and yanked him to safety.

On the other side, the group eyed the two ropes, knowing that at some point, they would have to make the return journey. This time, Hayden took point as they started off again. Now, the passage bent upwards a little, winding through the mountain.

Drake wondered how far they'd come. It had been a fair journey. He was still wondering when, all of a sudden, Hayden stopped. She stopped so suddenly, in fact, that everyone bumped into the person they were following.

Drake was half an inch from her back and managed to halt. He blinked in the confined space.

'What's happening?'

'I think there's a trap ahead.'

He peered over her shoulder. 'What is it?'

'Another dodgy looking rock. Pass the word.'

Drake saw it nestling in the path ahead. He made sure to turn and tell everyone what to watch out for and, soon, the entire group had gingerly passed the rock by. This time there was no spiked timber wall, and he wondered briefly what the trap might have entailed. Of course, he certainly didn't want to find out. He looked up and to the sides and examined the floor, but there was nothing obvious.

Hayden led the way for a while, and then Kinimaka took point. They followed the big Hawaiian as his shoulder sometimes brushed both sides of the tunnel, causing bits of rock to shear off and fall to the floor. It was a necessary slow procession. Drake felt sorry for Alicia, now the lone lookout at the back, because there was clearly no one following them. This wasn't that kind of mission. Her job was a bit redundant, and he knew she wouldn't enjoy being on her own back there with no one to take the piss out of.

He put his head down and continued. After a while, Mai went to the front and kept an eye out for traps, but no more came. The passage narrowed even more until they all found it difficult to navigate, especially Kinimaka and Dahl.

It was Mai who came to the end of the tunnel first and saw the surprise that awaited them.

CHAPTER THIRTEEN

A vast cavern opened out ahead, its rocky walls curved and high, its top festooned with rocky stalactites of all shapes and sizes. The floor was a jumble of rocks and boulders, barely a path between them. Through the centre ran a narrow stream, burbling along, picking its way through the chaos. The immense cave was a shock to the system after the endless stream of low, narrow passageways. The team fanned out and took a while to get used to it.

And then Drake's eyes fell upon something on the other side of the stream, something that nestled against the far wall of the cavern.

'Is that... ?' Danielle said.

But Kerry was already moving. 'Yes. Yes, it is.'

'Be careful,' Drake said, darting quickly to keep up with her.

They all moved towards the far wall, eyes filled with both shock and wonder. For there, perched on a smooth ledge, sat a large black altar. And on top of the altar sat a chest exactly the same as the one they'd found aboard the galleon.

'I didn't fully believe until now,' James, the other archaeologist, said.

All five of the aides agreed with him, but Kerry

was moving so fast Drake could barely keep up. She slotted her way through the boulders, large and small, unwary of traps. Drake had to shout to make her hear.

'Be careful,' he said. 'This is the perfect place for traps.'

Kerry slowed dramatically. She turned to him, eyes wide. 'Sorry,' she said softly. 'Just excited.'

He nodded. At last, he could take the lead again and thread a path through the jagged boulders. They neared the stream. He took his time. The stream was narrow enough to jump across. He leapt over warily, conscious of where his boots hit the rock on the other side.

'Everyone take the same path,' he said.

The way forward grew too tangled with rocks, and next, he found himself having to clamber over two of the bigger boulders. The climb phased none of them, and soon they were standing staring up at the black altar and its chest.

'I didn't allow myself to believe,' Kerry said. 'But there it is.'

Drake saw a carved altar, surprised by the nature of the carvings. Faces stretched in a rictus of pain. A dagger raised above a prone body. A demonic face screaming in pleasure. There were others too – men and women being stabbed to death and some vile creature eating a heart. Drake turned to stare at Kerry.

'These are the Cerberim?'

'They're not the easiest of people to get along with.'

'I'll say.'

'I bet nobody missed them when they were gone,' Hayden said.

Kerry's eyes now turned towards the chest. It was a quick climb up to the ledge where the altar waited. Drake went first, feeling for handholds carefully and testing each one before he committed. Soon, he was on the ledge, facing the altar. The chest was about head height.

Kerry came next, and then the other two archaeologists. There wasn't room for anyone else. Drake watched as Kerry reached out reverently for the chest. She took it carefully off the altar and laid it on the ground, then knelt before it. The archaeologists stared with bated breath.

'Do it,' Danielle said.

'My pleasure,' Kerry said.

She reached out, took hold of the lid and lifted. Drake was standing over her so saw what was inside first. It appeared to be a rolled sheet of paper.

'It's another scroll,' Kerry said. 'I think this is the next clue.'

'So we found it,' James said.

'We certainly did.' Danielle rose to her feet and punched the air, calling to the aides. 'We found it!'

There was a cheer that echoed around the cave. Drake smiled, as their excitement was infectious. Kerry reached into the chest and took hold of the scroll.

Drake watched intently. It was hard not to expect something nasty to happen. The traps they'd passed, and the carvings betrayed the nature of the Cerberim. He wouldn't put it past them to try something else.

But Kerry was okay. She pulled out the rolled up scroll and held it up before her. 'It's written in the same hand as the other,' she said. 'Same penmanship. This one is longer. Let us get our heads around it.' She paused and weighted it on the ground with rocks, sitting back so the others could see. Drake made way, since there was very little room up on the ledge, and let them work.

They idled their time away as the archaeologists did their jobs. Drake stared down at Hayden and Kinimaka and the others, watched them keeping an eye on the others, the way back, and the far entrance to the cave where Alicia currently stood. Alicia herself looked bored and was probably hoping for some attack of cave dwellers or something. Anything to stay active.

The archaeologists talked between themselves. They sat back on their knees, poured over the text. It took a while but, eventually, they climbed to their feet.

'I think we've got it,' Kerry said.

This time, Danielle held up the scroll. Drake noticed that one of the aides, the one named Lee, had separated from the others and was about as close as he could get to the rocky ledge. Eagerness glinted in his eyes.

Danielle said, *'From the diamond bay, travel east to the seven rock inlet. Continue east for two leagues and then go north to the rainbow waterfall. East of the waterfall is a lake and then the heart-shaped beach. This is your only route to find it. Find the rock pile with the horns and the small pool and dig inside.'*

Drake tried to take it all in. His memory wasn't great, especially after getting knocked on the head by enemies thousands of times. But he didn't have to remember it all; he knew the archaeologists and probably Hayden would take care of that.

'We have our instructions,' Kerry said. 'We should get out of here and follow them. First, we're returning to the diamond bay.'

'But at least we're staying on the island,' James said. 'It could be much worse.'

'For now,' Kerry said. 'For now.'

Drake watched her roll the scroll up carefully and place it in her backpack. The chest was passed down, put into a spare, and hefted by one of the aides. Kerry looked longingly at the altar.

'It's too heavy for now,' Drake told her. 'We'll come back for it.'

'We must. It's a historical object of the Cerberim. Few of them exist.'

'We will,' Drake said. 'Make note of the placement of the traps, though, so they don't snag the next group that comes here.'

He made his way back down and faced Hayden. 'What do you think?' He said. 'This is far less dangerous than our usual job.'

She nodded. 'I'm enjoying the peace and quiet,' she said. 'At the same time as missing the pure adrenalin. It's an odd combination.'

'It's dogfight withdrawal,' Kinimaka said. 'That's what it is.'

Drake smiled, then turned to look around. The atmosphere was relaxed. Dahl was talking to Kenzie and Mai. Alicia leaned against the far wall, a faraway look on her face. Kerry was talking to her fellow archaeologists, and the aides were all talking amongst themselves. Except Lee, he noticed. Lee kept to himself for now.

They took a brief break to give themselves sustenance for the long walk back. They all sat on the boulders, feet dangling, eating and drinking and thinking about the new clue. Kerry recited it aloud three or four times until even Drake could remember it. Alicia didn't join them, staying near the far wall. Drake didn't really expect her to since she was on lookout, but he couldn't help but miss her playful repartee.

They moved out. It was a long journey back, and they'd not exactly marked where the traps were, so had to be extra careful. They did that now by using cairns of stones so that the next set of explorers would have every chance to avoid them. It was a tougher journey as they were mostly headed uphill, but eventually, Drake saw the crescent-shaped entrance to the cave and blessed daylight.

Fresh air and light greeted them. Drake gulped it in, thankful. Again, the group took a rest before starting on their journey back to the diamond-shaped bay. Drake and the others surreptitiously checked for any disturbances or footprints, finding nothing. Clearly, they were entirely on their own.

'It feels odd,' Mai said as they set off again. 'Not to be fighting, or being pursued. It doesn't feel right.'

'Aye, I know what you mean. Everything we do is usually dangerous. Well, let's be thankful we're not being shot at for once and enjoy it, eh?'

Mai nodded. Alicia, overhearing, pulled a grumpy face. She wasn't happy.

'And to be fair,' Dahl put in, holding up a knife that looked comically small in his hand. 'It's not like we have a lot to fight anyone with. Using this,' he waved the knife. 'I wouldn't wager against the local rabbit population coming out on top.'

They started off back towards the diamond bay, guarding the others, staying alert and wary but encountering nothing suspicious. Maybe this time, Drake thought, they'd enjoy a peaceful mission.

Maybe...

CHAPTER FOURTEEN

Javier settled down in his plush seat, the stage offset to the left below him. The opera was about to begin, and he had the best seat in the house. The royal box, as it was called, sported gold filigree and gilded, tall candlesticks, a five tier chandelier just for show, and seats you could comfortably sleep in. Carpeting was thick and fluffy, and the lights were dimmed just enough. Javier had a waiter on hand; all he had to do was click his fingers, speak an order and the man would scuttle off. Javier did it now, ordering champagne, just because he could.

He leaned back. His family was with him tonight, filling the box left and right. Below, the orchestra was tuning up, the stage lighting was being managed and extras were sorting out last-minute details. Javier checked his watch. Ten minutes to go.

The theatre was full, he saw, chairs rammed from top to bottom. The noise level was high too, so high he couldn't hear his own family speaking. It was lucky then that he heard the sound of his phone ringing.

He fished the device out of his pocket. His wife gave him a sidelong glance, but he ignored it. Business was business.

'Hello? Hello?'

He couldn't hear the tinny voice on the other end of the line. Javier rose and then ducked out of the box, walking to a quieter passage that ran behind. In here it was dark and cool. He stopped to talk.

'Who is this?'

'Sir, it's Lee.'

'Lee?' For a moment, he couldn't place the man but belatedly remembered that he was the mole in that expedition. Something to do with the risen galleon, the Hellhound.

'This better be good,' he said.

'It is, sir. It is. It's all *real*.'

Javier blinked. 'What's all real? The treasure?'

'You remember they found the first chest, the one with the clue to the Cerberim's island and this place called the Underworld?'

It was all coming back to Javier now. He'd had a hundred different things to deal with since then and had almost forgotten about the Hellhound. 'The Underworld is where they hid their riches, right?'

'Yes, sir, that's it. You sent me with the expedition's aids in search of the first clue, just in case it turned out to be real. Well, sir, they found a second chest. A second clue. It's all real. The Underworld is out there somewhere.'

'With all the riches of a nation,' Javier said. 'I like the sound of that.'

'What do you want me to do, sir?'

'To my mind, we have two choices. We either follow them, let them do all the work until they eventually find this Underworld, which they may or may not do, and then take it all away from them. Or we eliminate any chance and look for it ourselves. I'm thinking the latter. You mentioned they have a team of guards. What are they like?'

'Pretty professional, sir. I'd say they're good.'

'It won't matter, but thanks for the heads up. You say they have the second clue. Have you read it?'

'Yes, sir, I can repeat it to you. *From the diamond bay, travel east to the seven rock inlet. Continue east for two leagues and then go north to the rainbow waterfall. East of the waterfall is a lake and then the heart-shaped beach. This is your only route to find it. Find the rock pile with the horns and the small pool and dig inside.*'

Javier nodded to himself, thinking about it. 'Send me a voice recording,' he ordered. 'I'll pass it along to Carlos. Lee, I want this second clue for myself. Delay them if you can. I can send a fast boat with six or seven armed men. Tell me, what weaponry do your guards have?'

Lee had already sent the voice recording, which also included instructions on how to find the island. Now he fell silent.

'Thinking about it, they appear to have only knives. I haven't seen a gun among them.'

Javier laughed. 'So much the better. Carlos will kill them all and leave their bodies to rot. Could the other aides and archaeologists prove useful?'

'At least two of the archaeologists are useful,' Lee said. 'They could be coerced into helping Carlos find the next clue.'

'I would trust him to do it without them, but you have a point. Using archaeologists might be useful.'

From somewhere down the passage, Javier heard

strident music start up. The opera had started. His wife would be livid.

He kept his attention on the job at hand. 'Well done, Lee,' he said. 'You have outdone yourself and will be rewarded. Stay on the inside, and call me with any information you can get.'

'Yes, sir, and thank you.'

Javier ended the call, and then immediately jabbed in another number. 'Carlos?' he said. 'I have a very important job for you. I need you and six or seven men – as many as you can fit into a fast boat – to go somewhere right now. I'm sending you the details.' He went on, explaining the whole Hellhound scenario in full. He told Carlos about the expedition, his man on the inside, the archaeologists and the guards. He mentioned the chests and the scrolls and the Cerberim, told Carlos of the Underworld. Soon, the man was all caught up.

Javier held his phone tight. 'You will get resistance,' he said. 'But I want you to crush it. Use any and all threats. We don't need prisoners, and can use some of the aides and guards as examples to keep the others in line. This island is uninhabited, so you will have free rein. Make use of it, and do not fail me. These guards are unarmed. No matter how good they are, you will defeat them and bring me the next clue. Is that clear?'

Carlos had barely spoken a word yet. But his deep voice resonated with confidence. 'Completely clear, boss. No mistakes. I understand perfectly and will pick the men with success in mind.'

'Good, and you can start out right now?'

'Of course, boss. We just have to find the island

and then start out looking for this next clue. Of course, that will take several hours, so we may be a bit behind.'

'I have asked Lee to delay them. Failing that, he's still undercover, and we might be able to get to the next clue faster. I understand you're playing catch up. Just do what you can, Carlos.'

'I'll get the men and the guns, boss. In that order. Nobody will stop us.'

'And if you can, use the archaeologists to help you solve these clues. It will be faster. I don't care what happens to them once their use comes to an end.'

'Not a problem, boss.'

'And Carlos?'

'Yes?'

'If possible, I want to be there at the end. If you get any warning, I want to be there when you go into the Underworld.'

'I understand.'

'Good, now get on with it and keep me informed.' Javier ended the call with a jab of a button. He'd never thought the Hellhound angle would pay this kind of dividend. It was lucky he was happy to diversify, to try anything. He was immensely pleased with himself.

He thought about the explorers, currently happy following their little trails, sitting around their campfires and making merry. Their lives were about to change, and not for the good. Javier smiled at that. He liked the idea of bringing war and violence to them, of making chaos out of peace. It was what he was born to do.

Smiling, he went back to the opera and his family.

CHAPTER FIFTEEN

On the way back to the diamond-shaped beach, Kerry made sure to read the clue out loud once more.

'From the diamond bay, travel east to the seven rock inlet. Continue east for two leagues and then go north to the rainbow waterfall. East of the waterfall is a lake and then the heart-shaped beach. This is your only route to find it. Find the rock pile with the horns and the small pool and dig inside.'

Drake was only half-listening, preferring to let the archaeologists do their own thing. He knew Kerry was more than an archaeologist – she was a researcher, a historian and a treasure hunter all rolled into one. But it was clear that she loved her job, and that she loved treasure hunting. She was a no-nonsense go-getter, and Drake liked her. He supposed her penchant for always having to be certain of something before stating a fact could be frustrating, but it was also endearing. She had character. And, to be fair, the other two archaeologists were good at their jobs too. Drake checked on James' minor wound, but saw nothing to concern him.

The team, apart from Kenzie, who was on perimeter guard duty, all gathered close as they walked.

'I'm bored,' Alicia said.

Drake sighed. 'What a team,' he said. 'Complaining because they *don't* have bullets flying around their arses.'

'It's a relatively short job,' Hayden said. 'And we have another one booked in about two weeks. Take the rough with the smooth.'

'Being Drakey's girlfriend, that's a given,' Alicia said. 'And that there's more rough than smooth.'

Drake sighed.

'And it's a paid gig,' Kinimaka put in. 'Pays the rent.'

'Not only that,' Hayden said. 'But it will put us in good stead with the archaeology crowd. If we get some word of mouth going, that'll be great for the future.'

Alicia had to nod her head at that. 'Good point.'

'Are we enjoying our return to treasure hunting?' Drake asked, negotiating a sprawling bush that stood in their way.

Alicia's response was obvious. The others all nodded. 'Minus the traps,' Mai said. 'I didn't like them.'

'And the rock climbing,' Alicia said. 'Not my idea of fun.'

'Oh, come on,' Dahl said. 'It was exhilarating.'

'Just go back to making your flat pack furniture,' Alicia sniffed at him. Dahl shook his head at her.

It took some time but, by late afternoon, they walked on to the diamond beach. Kerry and the others read the clue again and got their bearings whilst everyone grabbed snacks and a drink. Soon, the archaeologists were ready to set out.

'If we go now,' Hayden said. 'We're gonna have to pitch tents in the forest or wherever. We won't get there and back before nightfall.'

Kerry shrugged. 'I'm game. That's why we brought all the camping gear.'

The consensus was that they set out right away. For this leg of their journey, Kerry led the way, sticking closely to the directions offered by the scroll.

'We go east,' she said. 'To find the seven rock inlet.'

They took a direct course from the bay, finding themselves amongst the forest almost instantly. Dahl and Kinimaka moved to clear a path through for the others, who followed at a more sedate pace. The sun was past its zenith but still beat down hard and soon they were all sweating, covered in leaves and branches and dirt, and turning their faces often towards a most welcome sea breeze. The canopy kept the worst of the sun off, but it was still sweltering.

Darkness came sooner than expected. As they walked, shadows started creeping in, enhanced by the overhead tree cover. Drake began to make noises about finding a clearing where they could pitch their tents, but it was still another half hour until they actually found one. Once they did, the entire team set about pitching tents and laying canvas on the ground, setting up cooking implements, and lighting a fire. The fire wasn't absolutely necessary, but one of the aides said it would 'promote the joy of living outside.' The same aide, a man named Jed, was a competent chef, and skipped the erection of the mini tent city to start cooking them all a meal. By the time darkness fell, and Drake was ready to take a break, the smells coming from the cook fire were mouth watering. As darkness landed, the heat abated, and it became much more comfortable. Kenzie came in from her guard duties and Mai went into the forest as the team made sure their tents were as comfortable as they could be. Everyone was sharing, a fact which produced a few unhappy faces among the aides. Soon, the chef was ready to serve and brought forward a meal of rice, meat and veg, the ingredients of which he'd brought from their boat. He also produced a few bottles of wine.

'You dragged that all the way down the cave and back?' Alicia asked him in surprise.

'It's *wine,*' he answered. 'I wasn't going to leave it at the entrance for someone to steal.'

'No danger of that,' Drake said with a sigh. 'We're the only ones on this island.'

'Oh, so says the almighty,' Alicia said. 'How can you be sure?'

Drake thought about it. 'Just a feeling,' he said. 'Of emptiness. Abandonment. Desolation. Whoever once called this place home is long gone.'

A breeze wafted through the camp and flattened the fire's flames for a moment. Drake heard it whistling through the trees. This was a lonely old place, and he didn't really like it. The thought of old ghosts plagued the mind. At that moment, Jed came around offering red wine in plastic cups, and Drake shrugged off any negative thoughts. 'I didn't realise we were so well stocked,' he said.

'There's always room for wine,' Jed said, drinking.

'Ya got any bourbon in your bag of tricks?' Alicia asked.

Jed quickly produced a small bottle and handed it over. Alicia gave him a joyful look. 'Oh, man, I think I love you.'

'A bottle of bourbon?' Kenzie said. 'You're easy.'

'I never said otherwise.'

Alicia swigged the bourbon from the bottle without offering it around. Drake was happy with his wine, especially when Jed produced a second bottle. He wondered if Jed's entire pack contained alcohol. To be fair, he thought, it wasn't a bad way to travel.

Mai returned for food a bit later, and then wandered off again, saying she didn't mind taking the night shift. Drake was aware of her deep grief at the loss of Connor Bryant. It would never go away and didn't appear to be fading at all. He worried for her privately, but she was still performing perfectly professionally.

'You should talk to her,' Alicia said quietly.

Drake was surprised. 'You think? I wasn't sure how she'd take it.'

'You're her oldest friend. You should go find her.'

Drake found himself stalking through the forest, picking his way through the dark. He found Mai after a few minutes, and of course, she'd heard him coming.

'I have a knife pointed at your throat,' she said.

'I'd expect nothing less.' He nodded and decided to get straight to it. 'How are you, Mai?'

'I'm fine. You?'

He shook his head. 'You know what I mean.'

'Is there a problem?'

Maybe he was going about this the wrong way. 'No problem at all,' he said. 'But you haven't spoken about Bryant. At all. I know how much he meant to you.'

He couldn't see her eyes in the dark, but he felt her shift. 'I am lost,' she said. 'My heart is broken. But I can cope.'

'You don't have to cope alone.'

'It's hardly a team mission to make sure Mai's okay.'

Drake touched her shoulder. 'But it is,' he said. 'It's actually our most important mission. We all care for you beyond anything imaginable. And to see you hurting alone...' he sighed. 'I just want you to know that we're always there.'

'I miss him,' Mai whispered. 'Things were getting better and better, you know? At first, it was cagey, but as the months flew by. We understood each other. I just can't believe he's gone.'

Drake put an arm around her and hugged her close. He said nothing, but became a rock for her in that warm, dark place, became everything she needed to cling to. Mai cried, and Drake was there for her, forever if need be.

They stayed in the dark together for most of the night, whispering or in total silence. By the time the sunrise started filtering warmly through the trees, Drake and Mai were ready to return to the group.

'I know it'll never be right,' Drake said. 'But remember, you have people who care about you, who want to help if they can. Just remember, you're never alone.'

Mai nodded, a small smile on her face. The duo returned to the camp just in time to eat a cooked breakfast and consume lots of hot coffee. Jed was a speedy master around the cook fire.

Quickly, the team packed up their gear and stored it away. Then, they set off again, moving through the forest and then coming out of it to see a series of folding hills ahead. The going got much easier, and they crossed the hills with ease. Drake listened to the landscape as he walked, automatically alert to any kind of noise that didn't quite fit. Dahl ranged around their perimeter, keeping watch. The whole team was always on alert, always ready, with the archaeologists and the aides walking alongside them.

The shape of the coastline brought the sea closer as the day wore on, and soon they found themselves walking carefully along a cliff edge, following a path. Drake wondered if it had been worn centuries ago by the feet of the Cerberim. Nobody else had walked here in centuries. The coastline twisted away and then returned, and soon they were headed downwards. After a while, Kerry stopped, shielding her eyes to stare ahead.

'It's there,' she said.

People crowded around. Drake stared. Ahead, a small cove delved inland and, at its head, a series of large, heavy rocks stood, one on top of the other. They didn't form a shape, didn't look like anything at all, but there were seven of them.

'The seven rock inlet,' Danielle said. 'We need to get down to it.'

They wasted no time reaching the landmark and were soon crowded around. Kerry once again reminded them of the clue, and the next step. 'Measure two leagues east and then go north to find the rainbow waterfall,' she said. 'Are you ready?'

They were. One of the aides took out a distance

measuring device so they could be entirely accurate, and then they set off.

Drake exchanged a glance with Mai. 'Closer and closer,' he said.

CHAPTER SIXTEEN

Two leagues passed quickly. After that, the team looked at their assorted compasses and headed north. Drake thought it amusing that almost every one of them took out a compass and checked it, as if some of them could be wrong.

The trek north was easy, just a long plain that was headed towards some distant high hills. Drake thought that might be their destination. The sun had vanished behind a series of rain clouds now, a blessed relief.

The party picked their way onwards. There was so much open space now that Dahl did not need to range further afield. They would see anyone coming a mile off. But there was no one. As Drake had said, the whole island was abandoned.

Some time passed. The high hills ahead drew closer and closer, and eventually, they started to walk among them. Up and down the slopes and passed great boulders and piles of rock. It was only a matter of time before they found the waterfall.

And suddenly it was there, tumbling off a high hill and plunging down into a small lake. The rainbow effect didn't come from the sun though, it came from the multi coloured rocks at its base. They were different hues – reds and blues and yellows. All shimmering behind the endlessly falling water.

'The rainbow waterfall,' Kerry said.

'What's next?' Hayden asked.

'East to a lake and then a heart-shaped beach,' Kerry said, and turned around, wiping her brow. 'Let's go.'

They moved on, taking little time to admire the spectacular waterfall. Their route took them among the high trees again and soon they were walking along in semidarkness as the tree cover became total. It was about this time when Danielle, in the lead, halted.

'Oh, my god,' she said.

Drake was instantly at her side. 'What do you see?'

'A wall.'

He blinked in confusion. 'A what?'

'It's part of a wall. Look,' and now Kerry and James were crowding around. 'It's the side of a structure.'

Drake took a closer look. They had indeed stumbled across a crumbling wall. When he looked again, he saw other structures too, dotted among the trees, all overgrown and broken down. Kerry, Danielle, and James walked off at such a pace that they left the others behind.

'Don't go too far,' Drake said. 'Don't wanna lose you in here.'

'It's incredible,' Kerry said. 'At a guess, I'd say we've found the city of the Cerberim.'

The archaeologists spent some considerable time poking about the old ruins, finding what they thought were houses and perhaps a temple. They found a few old statues too, attached to walls and various steps and carved pillars. As if to prove Kerry right, the pillars were decorated with fanciful carvings of evil gods, vile deeds, and screaming men.

'Even on its own, this is a fantastic find,' Kerry said. 'A lost people, a lost city. This all has to be documented.'

'Well, it's not going anywhere,' Alicia said in her own inimitable way. 'So, shall we move on?' Eager to be done with the dull mission.

It took Kerry and the other two archaeologists a while to calm down enough to leave the new city behind. After a while, though, they got their bearings and moved on, picking their way through the extensive ruins and then leaving them behind. Drake guessed they had lost about two hours, but understood why. The new find would be greeted enthusiastically in certain circles around the world.

They continued east and eventually left the forest behind. Now, they were headed back towards the coastline and continually looking for a heart-shaped beach. It was around lunchtime when they finally found it.

The team looked down from a low cliff, and they were right on top of it. It was a simple task to find a way down the cliff, following a twisting path, and soon they were on the beach, which was a wide patch of sand set way back from the sea. The beach was surrounded by low cliffs and a sun trap. Drake estimated it was about two hundred feet wide.

Which meant the thing they were looking for was easy to spot.

Kerry saw it straight away, stopped, and pointed. Drake followed her arm. It wasn't just a rock pile, as the clue had said. It was a vast heap of rocks and stones and boulders that stood about twenty feet high, nestling under the cliff face as if hiding.

Kerry started walking towards it. Following the clue, she soon found the small pool beside it. 'Not exactly small,' she said, kneeling at the edge. The pool was about ten feet by ten and full of murky water. 'Do we dig *in* it, or around it?'

'There's enough of us to do both,' Drake said. 'Time to break out the shovels.'

As they did so, Drake stood back and took another look at the rock pile. He'd been so intent on looking for the clue that he'd failed to spot the horns on top, but now that he stood back and took a long look, he felt the hairs on the back of his neck rise.

The heap of stones appeared to have horns curling from the top, horns that reminded Drake of pictures of the Devil. It was truly a spine-tingling sight and, as he looked on, he felt afraid for the people working under the very shadow of the curved horns.

Was it a bad omen?

He tried to shake it off.

CHAPTER SEVENTEEN

Drake turned away from what he was already thinking of as the demon's head.

The team had produced all their shovels and was looking at Kerry for direction. The archaeologist had as much idea as they did where the next chest might be found, so just shrugged.

'Just start digging,' she said. 'We need a volunteer for the pool.'

One of the aids stepped forward, shrugged out of most of his clothes and stepped in. Soon, he was rooting around the bottom of the pool and asking for a shovel. It was blind work, but there wasn't much else he could do. Around the edges, the others started digging too, throwing piles of sand back against the cliff face. Drake and his team helped and since cliffs and sea water surrounded them, they didn't post a sentry this time. There seemed little point. Soon, everyone was hard at work.

Drake tried not to think about the shadow that he worked in. One by one, the others had taken a look too, and come back shivering, and Kerry was currently staring at the phenomenon with wide eyes. Drake dug another shovel full of sand and threw it into a corner. Around the pool, the others worked, and soon a large hole developed to all sides.

With the whole crew working, people were everywhere and hard to keep track of. Drake wondered if maybe they should have someone watching from afar just to keep an eye on everyone, but just then, there was a scream.

'Help!'

Drake looked toward the noise. He saw a woman, an aide, floundering in the sand. The scene didn't look right, and he felt confusion, but ran hard towards it anyway, gradually realising what was going on.

The woman had stepped into quicksand and was sinking fast. Mai and Kenzie reached her first, threw themselves to their knees, and thrust their hands out. The woman grabbed hold and tried to pull herself free, but the sand was strong and she was sinking inexorably. Mai and Kenzie both tried pulling, but couldn't find the right leverage. All they did was to arrest the woman's descent.

Drake reached Mai and then Alicia reached Kenzie. They both grabbed the women around the waists and hauled back. The woman was screaming constantly and struggling, which only made her plight worse, but Drake didn't really blame her. He pulled Mai as hard as he could and hoped the Japanese woman could keep hold of the struggling aide.

Together, they dragged the woman out of the sand. She came squelching and filthy, her clothes covered in the clinging sand. All around now, the others were crowding around, wanting to help, but finding no room. The woman was gasping and coughing, crying out her thanks.

Drake sat back, exhausted. Mai lay next to him. The woman was prone, panting and just happy to be alive. There were several tense moments of mostly silence.

'From now on,' Dahl said eventually. 'We thoroughly vet an area.'

The thought of quicksand had never occurred to Drake. Knowing his luck, he'd have been looking around and then fallen headfirst into it. He sat up now and brushed himself off. It was going to be a long-ass day.

They dug and dug until well into the afternoon. The hole became huge, and the guy in the pool was joined by another. They brought sludge and slurry up, but stayed doggedly at their task.

It was an aide working at the top end of the pool whose shovel suddenly cracked against something solid. Everyone heard it. They all looked up. Dahl was closest and went immediately to his side. Together, the two of them knelt in the sand and cleared it with their hands, trying to expose the object. So far, they had all encountered hidden rocks and tree roots and just assumed this might be another.

And then Dahl exposed the sharp edge of something that could only be the chest. It was situated right between the horns at the top of the pool, an area Drake should have guessed would be an obvious choice. Minutes passed as Dahl and the aide swept away sand from the side of the chest and totally exposed it.

'It looks just the same,' Kerry said excitedly and unnecessarily.

'It is the same,' Dahl said. 'It's exactly what we're looking for.'

They lifted the chest out of the hole and carried it to a small pile of flat rocks. Dahl positioned it on top and then stood back, waiting for Kerry. The archaeologist wasted no time walking up to the object and studying it first from the outside.

'Usual carvings,' she said. 'Do you see?'

Behind them, Mai and Kenzie were still helping the woman who'd almost drowned in the quicksand. She had walked to the water, taken off her clothes, and was trying to clean them and her hair and face. Drake felt sorry for her.

Kerry finished her examination of the box. 'Only one thing left to do,' she said.

'Open it,' Danielle said.

With reverence, Kerry reached out both hands.

CHAPTER EIGHTEEN

The chest opened, its lid coming up to reveal what was inside.

Drake was standing close to Kerry, so got a good look before anyone else. It wasn't a surprise. Nestled inside the chest was another scroll, this one rolled up. Kerry dug inside, unrolled the scroll, and held it up to the light.

Everyone gathered around as she spoke.

'Sail twenty leagues back to find the island of tall peaks. Go to the church and search under the old basement to find the chest.'

'That seems straightforward enough,' James said. 'We should be able to find that, no problem.'

'It means us leaving the island,' Kerry said with some reluctance.

'Not for long,' James said. 'Once we've found the Underworld and the treasure, we can return to the ruins.'

Kerry nodded. 'Yes, they will wait for us. And we need to find the Underworld. Then now, I guess we should head back to the boat.'

That appeared to be the consensus all around. Drake thought about the trek back. If his bearings were right, they were just up the coast a bit from the diamond-shaped beach. Not far at all.

'I think less than an hour should do it,' he said. 'Assuming my inner navigator is working properly.'

'Then let's-' Kerry suddenly stopped talking. Her mouth fell open.

'Who the hell is that?' One of the aides said.

Drake had been concentrating on Kerry. Now he turned around. Seven men were hurrying down the side of the cliff, following the curving path. With alarm, Drake saw they were armed.

'Not so abandoned after all,' Dahl said.

'Unless they've only just arrived,' Hayden said.

'But how would they know to come right here?' Kinimaka murmured.

The seven armed men made their way to the bottom of the cliff. Once there, they started towards the explorers, taking their time. The man in front had a harsh, stern face and long hair and never once took his eyes off the group. Drake and the Ghost Squadron fanned out, moving away from each other and nearer where, all being well, the seven men would stop. Their hands were close to their knives, but they did not yet know the newcomers' intentions. Also, the men had not yet raised their weapons.

The two groups became one as the seven men approached, stopping just metres away. They were a ragtag bunch, wearing an assortment of t-shirts and jeans and shorts and hoodies. Their clothes were dirty and ripped as though they wore them often, their hands bruised and scarred. These men were no strangers to violence.

Drake moved to the head of the group.

'Hello,' he said equably, wondering if they spoke English.

Dahl pushed him aside. 'I think you should let someone without a silly accent do the talking,' he said, then repeated. 'Hello.'

'I am Carlos,' the leader with the long hair said. 'You will give us the scroll.'

'What scroll?' Drake said, wondering just how much they knew.

'The one you just took from the chest,' Carlos said threateningly. 'It is ours.'

'How do you know about the scroll?' Kerry said.

'That does not matter. Now, hand it over.'

Carlos took another step forward. He was very close to Drake now. The other members of the Ghost Squadron were close to their own would-be opponents. But were they close enough?

Not yet.

Drake stopped Kerry from handing the scroll over by holding out his own hand. 'Give it to me,' he said.

Kerry's eyes narrowed, but she placed it in his hand.

Drake turned to Carlos. 'Why do you want this?' He was still fishing for information.

Which Carlos was only too happy to give. 'To find out the clue, of course. And follow it to the Underworld.'

So they knew everything, Drake thought. How? Where had these men come from? Where were they getting their information?

He looked at the scroll. 'There isn't a lot on here,' he said.

His team was inching closer and closer to its opponents. It wouldn't be long now. He wondered idly who had missed this recently. Alicia, for sure. He could see the big smile plastered across her face.

Carlos reacted in anger and brought his gun up. Drake had pushed him a bit too far. 'Just give me the damn scroll. *Now.*'

Drake shrugged and held it out. Carlos grinned and dropped the weapon, holding his hand out to take the scroll. As he did, in that vulnerable position, Drake struck. He punched Carlos in the throat and then the eyes, and then grabbed the gun arm. He stepped around, wrenching the weapon free and seeing it fall to the ground. Carlos swung too, moving with Drake to prevent his arm from being broken.

The others struck at the same time. Mai stepped into her opponent, kneeing him between the legs and snatching his weapon away. Kinimaka brought a haymaker around, laying his enemy out without the slightest sound. Kenzie and Alicia both chose to leap on their opponents and wrestle them to the ground, neutralising their gun arms. Dahl quickly stepped around his man and tripped him, then landed a heavy boot on the man's sternum. Hayden grabbed her man's gun first, twisting it from his hand and breaking a thumb.

Carlos' group of mercs was stunned, but weren't out of the fight. They knew conflict and struggle. They fought back, quickly trying to regain the upper hand.

Drake let Carlos swing around and then elbowed him in the face. Carlos grunted but kept coming. Drake kicked the gun away. Carlos swung at him, face bloody. Drake blocked and then kicked out, landing his boot on Carlos' chest. The man staggered away, but that didn't stop him. He dived headlong for the gun.

Drake met him with another kick, this one directed at his face. Carlos hit it head on, and yelled out in pain, then rolled in the dirt, facing the sky. He coughed, his face now running with blood. Drake reached down and picked up the gun.

'Don't move.'

Around the beach, the Ghost Squadron was fighting hard. Alicia cut her opponent down with expert precision, wasting no time targeting nerve endings and muscle masses and eyes and ears. The man was on his knees within seconds, gasping, holding his head. Alicia stood over him with his gun in her hand, already looking for the next opponent. Mai was similar, wiping her enemy out with consummate skill, leaving him writhing in the sand. All this time the archaeologists and aides stood back, watching with their mouth open, some crouching down in case a bullet went off. Dahl battered his aggressor from all sides, fists flying until the man didn't know which way up he was standing. Kinimaka lifted his man by the jacket and flung him into the nearest rock pile.

By now, the Ghost Squadron had all the guns. They levelled them at the mercs and now it was their turn to ask the questions.

Drake aimed his gun at Carlos. 'How did you know about the scrolls?'

Carlos spat in the sand at Drake's feet.

Drake ratcheted a round into the gun so that Carlos could see he knew what he was doing. 'Answer the question,' he said. 'What do you know about the scrolls?'

Carlos prepared another mouthful of spit, so

Drake just slammed him in the nose with the butt of the rifle. Carlos' eyes went wide and pain stretched the features of his face. He held his nose, gasping.

Around the beach, the Ghost Squadron was conducting similar enquiries. So far, none of the motley crew had folded. Drake weighed their options. The archaeologists and the aides were all watching. He didn't want to go too far. Also, he wasn't about to kill these men in cold blood, despite what might have happened if the tables were turned.

And when he looked around, Hayden was looking at him. He could tell by the look in her eyes and years of experience that she was thinking exactly the same thing. He nodded.

'Get out of here,' she told them. 'We'll hang on to your weapons. Just turn around and go, whilst you still can.'

Carlos looked surprised. His eyes narrowed, as if expecting a trap. But Drake waved the gun at him. 'Go,' he said. 'I'm not gonna murder you.'

'But you come at us again,' Dahl added. 'Armed. The outcome might not be quite so nice.'

Carlos led his men away from the beach and started walking back up the slope. Drake turned to the archaeologists. 'Everyone okay?'

Kerry and the other two nodded, though they all looked nervous. 'What do you think's going on?' Kerry asked.

'I think someone with resources has got wind of the Hellhound Scrolls,' Drake said. 'And I don't think that's the last we're gonna see of our new friend, Carlos.'

'Only they won't be taken by surprise next time,' Dahl said.

'Good,' Alicia muttered. 'Because that was no fight at all.'

Kenzie nodded her agreement. 'Two minutes and done,' she said, shaking her head.

'Oh, I've had shorter sessions,' Alicia said. 'Wait... are we still talking about fighting?'

Drake thought it best that they should get moving. He didn't want Carlos and his men to come up with any ideas or maybe even locate more weapons. They were here to protect the archaeologists, but he didn't really want a shootout.

'Let's get back to the boat,' he said.

CHAPTER NINETEEN

Kerry sat on the boat as the pilot motored them away, exercising caution until they were far enough away from the beach not to be seen. He stayed level with the island, though, because he'd been told there were a certain amount of leagues to follow toward the next clue. Kerry perched on a stool in the main cabin with the others all lounging around her. So far, this had been an eventful operation. They had progressed further than she could have hoped in so short a time, but she didn't want to count her chickens yet. She still exercised the reserve she was famous for among certain circles. When someone said they were doing well, she returned the smile with a slight shake of her head. *Maybe.*

Inside, though, she was elated. She was finding it hard to keep a lid on her enthusiasm. At first, she'd barely believed the scrolls, and the Cerberim were real. That anything would be found at all. But finding that first chest had energised her beyond measure. It was *all* real.

She drank water from a bottle and leaned back. The entire team was here, including the bodyguards. She had been impressed back on the beach at the way they'd handled those armed men. Impressed and scared. She was so glad she'd hired them. What would have been the outcome if the Ghost Squadron weren't present?

Would she be dead now?

Kerry shrugged it off. But it was hard to let go. Carlos hadn't seemed the type to back down. He would be back, commanded no doubt by someone who knew exactly what was going on. She listened to her team talk, running through events. The main topic was who were those men and how had they found them?

The only explanation was that there was a spy in their midst.

Kerry watched the team come and go, some visiting the bathroom, others going to get air or go for a walk around the deck. Was someone here working against her? She didn't want to believe it, but what other explanation was there? She looked at the scroll in her hand and wondered what to do next.

And yet, still, she wasn't sure. She wasn't part of a nasty, traitorous world. She wanted to believe in the best of her fellow companions. That they were all on each other's side. Trust among treasure hunters was important, she thought with a small smile. They were forced to rely on each other.

Now... more than ever.

Lee took the first opportunity to take a toilet break. He laughed and emoted with the group, showed that he was one of them, and then left them behind to lock himself away and betray them.

Sitting on the toilet, he took out his phone and

pressed a speed dial number. Soon, the call was answered.

'Hello?'

'Javier, is that you?' He whispered.

'Who else would it be?' Javier sounded angry.

Lee swallowed hard. 'Your men failed at the beach. They failed to get the clue. But I heard the female archaeologist read it out loud, and have it memorised for you.'

Javier took a deep breath. 'Good. At least I can rely on one of you.'

Lee felt pride. 'Thank you. Did, umm, Carlos and the others make it clear?'

'Don't worry about Carlos and the others. That is my next call. I will deal with them. Just give me the next clue.'

Lee reeled it off as best as he could remember it. He was pretty certain he made no mistakes. It wasn't that hard.

'Is that it?' Javier asked. 'All of it?'

'Yes, that's it, I'm afraid.'

'Well, it's pretty succinct. Well done, Lee. Now keep your head down. We failed this time and those mercenaries she hired will know something's not right. They'll be wondering how we found them, for starters. Just do your job and keep a low profile. Take no unnecessary risks. I need you on the inside.'

Again Lee felt pride. Javier needed him. The words made him think of all the riches that would be headed his way once this mission was done. Javier was sure to reward him.

'You can rely on me,' he said. 'I'm your man.'

'Good,' and Javier ended the call.

Lee made his way back to the main cabin, smiling as his companions welcomed him back.

Javier bristled with anger and forced himself to sit and calm down. He felt like strangling something. Carlos had failed and had failed miserably. The idiots had even lost their weapons. The real downside was that now they had lost their element of surprise. These mercenaries knew they were coming.

Javier was currently sitting in his private office, well away from everyone else. It was quiet in here, meditative, and he liked it. There were no windows, just one door that was locked, and an enormous oak desk with a plush leather chair. He had communications and computers and everything else he wanted but, right now, he needed a drink to calm down.

If he didn't, he would probably order Carlos killed.

And he didn't want that. Carlos, despite today, was his best man and a good ally. Carlos actually cared about Javier's operation. And everyone was due a mistake sooner or later. Javier thought about the Hellhound operation. Was it all worth it? He had plenty of other campaigns going.

He considered the new clue Lee had given him. It was intriguing, like nothing else Javier was involved in. He actually wanted to take part himself, but wouldn't do that yet. They needed to be closer to their prize first.

But how close were they?

Javier forced himself to sit, to breathe, to take a

drink. He tried to empty his mind for a few minutes. The urge to kill slowly receded, draining into the background where it always lived. It never left him, but he could usually control it.

Finally, Javier picked up the phone. He dialled Carlos and waited a few moments for his second-in-command to answer.

'Hey, boss,' was the man's first words.

Javier bit his bottom lip until the blood flowed. 'You fucked up real bad, Carlos.'

Carlos' voice fell. 'Sorry, boss. They were better than expected and we were worse. It won't happen again.'

'They stole your weapons and sent you away with your tails between your legs?'

Carlos had already told Javier all this. Javier was reiterating to help get his anger out of the way and show Carlos how close he was to death. 'Anyone else…' he said. 'If it was anyone else…'

'It won't happen again, boss. I'd rather die first.'

'You're lucky to be alive right now.'

Carlos clearly knew Javier didn't mean at the hands of his enemies. He meant by the word of his own boss. He remained quiet.

'Did you learn anything of use to us?'

Carlos cleared his throat. 'Only that the mercs they hired are good,' he said. 'Very good. All of them. I saw the scroll and the chest, but didn't lay hands on either. They surprised us, but it won't happen again.'

'I have the new clue for you, Carlos. Do not fuck it up this time. Do I have to come out there myself?'

'No, boss, that won't be necessary. I can handle this.'

'You'd better, Carlos. You'd certainly better.'

'We'll shoot first next time,' Carlos tried to lighten the mood.

Javier wasn't amenable to it. 'Except now they have weapons,' he snarled. '*Your* weapons. Now they can fire back. And if they're as good at shooting as they are at fighting... you guys are in real trouble.'

Javier wondered how Carlos would handle such a statement. Would he fold and ask for more men? Would he bully his way through? It was an interesting, loaded question.

Carlos seemed to sense it. He answered very carefully. 'We're better than they are,' he said. 'We'll prove it to you.'

'Good to hear. Now, are you ready for the next clue? Lee is working really well on the inside. Hasn't put a foot wrong. I wish I could say the same about you.'

'Ready for the clue, boss.'

Javier sat back and read it out to him, gave him time to copy it down. Carlos apologised again and then was gone. Javier wondered if he was doing right, putting all his trust in a man who'd just failed. It didn't sit well.

I should probably kill Carlos myself.

Later, though, he thought. After the man had worked his ass off to make up for his failure. That would be the best time to act.

The thought gave Javier a modicum of respite.

CHAPTER TWENTY

The boat sailed through smooth, glittering waters.

Kerry had made the decision to set them on their way in search of the next clue. Time wasn't on their side, and the faster they went, the less chance they had of running into the bad guys again. Or at least, that was the consensus. The aides broke out the GPS and measured the twenty leagues as Kerry re-read the clue.

'Sail twenty leagues back to find the island of tall peaks. Go to the church and search under the old basement to find the chest.'

Drake watched the leagues tick by. The GPS was very precise. He hoped the Cerberim's measurements were equally accurate. He set up a watch on deck, asked the others to monitor the islands they sailed past and the seas to their horizons. There was every chance they were being followed. Maybe that's how Carlos and his men had found them. It didn't seem plausible – they'd kept a small perimeter watch on the island – but he guessed it was possible. He wasn't deluded enough to think his team was perfect.

They were forced to stop when the sun went down – not wanting to miss their chance to see the tall peaks – and spend another night on the water. They'd only covered eight leagues by then, and anchored in the middle of the rolling waters. Drake made sure a watch was kept throughout the night, though, in the utter blackness, anyone could have crept up on them unseen until they attacked.

They spent a tense night barely sleeping and breakfasted the next morning as the captain got underway. Twelve leagues weren't far, and soon, Drake was out on deck with a mug of coffee in his hand, gazing to the west. They were passing a rocky, featureless island that looked almost flat. It had no beach and no bays to be seen and had probably been uninhabited forever. Drake wondered if any human had ever set foot there.

The boat cut through the pearlescent waters. It was another bright sunny day, though there were rain clouds in the sky. Drake hoped they'd drift away, but they started to get thicker and closer.

'We may have to contend with that today,' he said, nodding at them.

The others were crowded around, except Dahl and Mai, who were watching land and sea. 'We've been lucky so far,' Hayden said. 'Maybe we'll get it done quick.'

Drake was minded to ask her not to tempt fate. He was sure the other team wouldn't be ahead of them. After all, they all needed daylight to find the tall-peaked island in accordance with the clue. And they were moving fast.

The flat island fell behind, and then they were looking ahead to the next island. One of the aides, Jed, was staring hard at the GPS. 'Nineteen leagues,' he said. 'We're close.'

Drake shaded his eyes and looked ahead to the next island. It was already in sight and, straight away, Drake could see that it was anything but flat.

'Are those tall peaks?' Kinimaka said. 'I think so.'

The island slid by on their right. Drake saw several bays with beaches and a few trees close by but, beyond that, several tall spires jutted up towards the sky from the middle of the island. It was in sharp contrast to the island they'd just passed. Drake counted eight peaks, all ragged and craggy. The captain eased up on the engine, stopped the boat, and weighed anchor. Kerry walked to the right side of the boat.

Together, they lowered the smaller boats into the sea and started the engines. They motored to what appeared to be the easiest navigable bay, running their boats almost to the shore and then tying them up tightly. The full team had a lot of gear with them in their backpacks, and now Drake's team also had weapons. They didn't let down their guard for a moment, conscious that Carlos and his men would be back.

The beach was wide and flat, perfect for their purposes. Drake sent Mai and four others into the trees to scout the general area, looking for any signs of others. The team moved off cautiously.

Drake watched the archaeologists and aides get to work. They unpacked a large backpack and took out a silver drone. One of the aides picked up a control module and started fiddling with it, looking like he knew what he was doing. Drake walked over to Kerry.

'You gonna use the drone to find the church?'

'That's the idea.'

'I was wondering how you were planning to find a church on this island.'

'Tried and tested,' Kerry said. 'If it's here, we'll find it.'

Soon, the drone was ready. Drake listened as the perimeter team reported on the comms that all was well, and there were no signs of strangers. So far, so good. The drone whined as it lifted into the air, little propellers whirling. Drake watched it go up and then fly away over the trees at a slow pace. The aide used a remote to fly it, and others stared into a larger monitor, seeing what *it* was seeing.

Drake let them work. They all stood around in a half circle, most of them watching the monitor. He saw the flash of the drone somewhere up high as the sun hit its wings and then it was gone, circling away. The team had obviously done this before and knew exactly what they were doing.

Drake was restless. Yesterday's action had done little to alleviate the sense of idleness he was feeling. He had to constantly remind himself that they were here, doing something, earning their wages. And now there was a new sense of danger. The thought of Carlos' team. . .Drake wasn't sure if he welcomed it or was worried about it. After all, they had a lot of people to guard.

So far, it had all gone well. One archaeologist had picked up a minor injury in the cave and that was it. Nothing to fret over. Maybe this new venture — Spear Solutions — was viable, after all. He certainly hoped so. He didn't know how to do much else.

Several hours passed as the drone did its thing

and fed images back. Drake ate and drank and did a patrol through the thin forest. He came out on the other side, saw craggy rolling hills that led to the foot of the tall peaks. It was a barren landscape and, the closer the hills got to the peaks, the higher they became. He wondered about the placement of a church here. It would undoubtedly be old – perhaps belonging to a single ancient settlement?

Drake returned to camp, saw Alicia drinking water, sitting on a rock, her gun at her side, and walked over. They hadn't had any alone time recently and, to be fair, had spoken little beyond work.

'You okay?' Drake asked.

'Adjusting to real work,' Alicia said with a sigh. 'It feels different when you're having to earn a crust.'

'Are we good?'

She looked up at him. 'How do you mean?'

He sat on the rock beside her. 'You've felt distant these past few weeks,' he said. 'Things feel different. Is everything okay?'

'You know me,' Alicia laughed. 'Always searching for the next thing. The next mission, the next horizon, the next adventure. I've always been the same.'

Drake knew it, and didn't like the sound of her feelings. 'Are you saying you want to move on?' He meant from him, from the time, from their lives.

She turned quickly to him. 'Oh, no, not at all. Don't worry. You'll know if I get bored with you, Drakey.'

Still, he was worried about her. Alicia hadn't been her normal self for a while now, even though she tried hard to be. Maybe Mai's own sadness was affecting her. It might also be the change in job activities – the new business venture that none of them had ever done before. Change wasn't always what it was cracked up to be.

Drake himself was rolling with the changes. This new job would bring different roles and missions. All they had to do was adapt. Maybe that was the hard part.

'Well, I think we're gonna see more action before all this is over,' he said. 'That should cheer you up, at least.'

'I'm not sad, Drake. I don't know what I am, but it's not sad. If I wanted to be sad, I'd think about our recent past with Bryant and what happened to Cam and Shaw. My philosophy is always to look to the future, to move ahead. Move on. That helps stop the sadness from gathering.'

Drake nodded and looked over at the group of aides and archaeologists. Still, they were gathered around the monitor, staring intently. Still, nothing had happened. The drone had to have covered half the island by now. His team used their comms regularly to keep him updated.

Just then, one of the watching archaeologists cried out. It was James, and he jabbed at the screen. The others crowded round even tighter. There was a sudden, excited conversation. Drake watched them closely.

'That's it,' James was saying. 'Do you see?'

Kerry was close enough to the screen so that her nose was almost touching it. 'I do. Right on top of that hill.'

'We've found it,' Danielle said.

The aides seemed equally excited. Kerry stood back. 'Now, all we have to do is to plot a route,' she said. 'From here to the church.'

Drake drifted over for a look. The drone hovered over a high, green hill. The top was flat, and in the centre sat a structure. A simple steeple at one end with its stone cross signified what kind of building it was. Drake saw no other structures scattered around. The church appeared to be on its own. Quickly, he used the comms to alert his team to the find.

The archaeologists started plotting their route.

CHAPTER TWENTY ONE

The entire team set off on what could be an arduous trek. They started on the beach and were soon threading their way through trees. The sun was shining again; the rain clouds having passed over without incident. There was a pleasant sea breeze too, something Drake welcomed as the temperature rose.

They slotted through the mini forest and then found themselves on a wide, green plain. It led towards a series of rolling hills in the distance. Drake knew they were aiming for the third hill in line. Their own destination lay beyond that, a few leagues to the west. They had recalled the drone but could send it out again if they got confused. The Ghost Squadron were on full alert and Dahl had asked if they could use the drone to monitor the island's bays, just to check if they were about to get company. The archaeologists had agreed, and the aides were currently helping Dahl fly the thing as they walked. Dahl watched the monitor closely, checking everything.

Mai, Alicia and Kenzie were also out there, ranging the perimeter. So far, they had encountered no issues. Yes, they had an enemy, but that enemy was not here today. At least, not yet.

They traversed the long plain under the hot sun. The ground rolled and was quite scrubby in parts, tripping more than one aide. For most, it was a bit of a slog, but eventually they reached the first of the foothills.

They started up. It took a while to reach the top of the hill, and then they stopped for refreshment. Some of the aides grumbled they hadn't signed up for a walking trek. The archaeologists ignored them. To be fair, they, too, seemed winded.

Drake swigged water and took a bite to eat. Soon, they were on their way again, this time descending the hill. At the bottom of this hill lay the slopes of another, and then they were on their way up again, traversing hill after hill. Midday passed and then they were in to the afternoon. The aides were forced to use the drone again to make sure they were on the right path.

Finally, Kerry said, 'This is the hill.'

Everyone looked hopefully at her.

She nodded. 'Yeah, guys, this is it. The church should be at the top.'

With renewed vigour they started off. The trek wasn't long, but it was the end of an extended journey. Everyone was sweating and panting by the time they reached the top.

'Well, we know one thing,' Kerry said as they neared the summit. 'The priests who lived here were athletes.'

And then they topped the hill. Drake smiled to see the church building right in front of them. Kerry straightened and gave a little cheer.

'We made it,' she said.

CHAPTER TWENTY TWO

Drake studied the building that lay in front of them.

The church stood at the centre of a flat area of land atop the hill. It was an old ramshackle building, still intact, but showing the ravages of age. It looked clean, bleached by the sun, washed by thunderstorms, and stood out in its solitariness. There wasn't another brick building in sight.

Drake organised the perimeter as Dahl recalled the drone. They had seen no sign of others for the last half hour, but the island had so many bays and inlets it was hard to keep track of them all. Kerry led the archaeologists towards the church, the aides following. Drake could hear the excitement in their voices as they approached the church.

'Remember the clue?' James said.

'I do,' Danielle said. *'Go to the church and search under the old basement to find the chest.'*

'But how will we know where to look?' Kerry wondered.

'Part of the excitement,' James said a little moodily, marching at the head of the pack.

Drake joined then, along with a couple of the Ghost Squadron, leaving the rest to guard outside. He let the others go first and then followed along in their wake, leaving them to their work. James reached a wooden front door first and found it hanging off its hinges.

'It's still kind of attached,' Danielle said.

James pulled it wide open and signalled for Kerry to precede him. The archaeologist walked straight in, torch in hand. Drake waited his turn. At one point, there were so many people trying to get inside the church they had to form a queue. Finally, Kerry trimmed down the numbers and some disappointed aides waited outside. Drake was the last to enter.

He found himself in a large room. Pews lined the centre, old and wooden and dusty. There was an altar and a cross at the far side, the only light gleaming through several stained glass windows in bright shafts. The floor was dusty and littered with leaves that had blown in through gaps in the deteriorating block work. Drake saw a crypt to the left and a few niches to the right, two of which were occupied by statues. Kerry immediately walked over to the statues.

'Figures,' she said. 'Nothing special about them. Maybe they're saints. Nothing to tie this place to the Cerberim.'

Drake kept a sharp eye out. The place didn't look dangerous, and nothing appeared ready to collapse. The rafters above were sturdy and strong, and the walls were generally sound. He looked across at Mai and Kinimaka, who were also inside the church, the latter taking up a lot of space. They both looked bored, and were watching Kerry to see what she did next.

Drake did the same. Kerry took a few minutes to

study the inside of the church and then started looking for a way down to the basement. She didn't hang around too much. There was excitement shining in her eyes. She spied a door and marched over to it.

'Let's try this,' she said.

She took hold of the handle and pulled. The door scraped open. Beyond, she saw a set of stone stairs leading into darkness. She shone her flashlight down and then turned around.

'I think we've found the basement,' she said.

'Let us go first,' Drake said.

He stepped forward, shone his flashlight down, and illuminated a straight set of concrete stairs. They were dusty, concave in the middle. He started down slowly with Mai at his back.

The air was musty. Dust motes span in the light of the torch. All he could hear were the boots of the others following him, and their collective breathing. The walls were brick and rough to the touch. He counted the steps as he descended. Twelve, and then he was standing on the basement floor.

He shone the torch around. The basement was empty, the floor just bare wooden planking.

'There's not a whole lot to look at,' he said. 'And be careful. Some of those planks might be rotten.'

But the archaeologists were excited beyond measure. They hit the basement running, chasing from wall to wall and studying the floors. They got the aides looking too, everyone scouring every surface. When Drake asked, Kerry told him they weren't exactly sure what they were looking for, but they'd know when they found it.

He stepped back, let them work. Half an hour later, Kerry was proven right as one of the aides let out a cry of triumph. She had been bent double, staring at the floor, and now she stood upright, beckoning Kerry over.

The archaeologist practically ran to her side. Next, Drake saw, almost everyone was bent over, staring at the floor. He decided to join them.

'What's happening?' he said.

Kerry didn't look up, but answered with eagerness in her voice. 'The floor, underneath the dust layer,' she said. 'Right here. It has a carving, just like the ones on the galleon.'

Drake peered harder. Sure enough, he saw a snarling face with horns and slanted eyes. 'Looks like a demon,' he observed.

'Probably one of the gods they worshipped,' Kerry said. 'To me, though, this says the chest is under here. Under the floorboards.'

Drake nodded. 'You could be right. The carving is X marks the spot.'

The team set about removing the floorboards around the carving. They wasted no time. Drake watched them work, nodding in appreciation. Soon, they had several planks up and were peering into a dusty hole. As he'd expected, Kerry's head was the furthest inside.

'Something's here,' she said, grunting.

She reached in further, straining, and then pulled. She same up with a chest in her arms and a grin on her face. 'I think we found it.'

Drake watched her lay the filthy object on the floor. Those around her watched with enthusiasm in their eyes. A hush fell over them, and many of them held their breath.

Kerry unfastened the chest and lifted the lid. Drake was able to see inside. There was a yellowed sheet of paper, a scroll, rolled up. Kerry pulled it out and held it up to the light. Drake saw scratchy black writing.

'This is it,' she said. 'The next clue.'

'What does it say?' Mai asked, herself getting caught up in the moment.

'In Singapura is the ancient ceremonial temple called Pulau Ujong. In the eastern wall find the symbol and the chest.' Kerry read it out reverentially, as if reciting a prayer. When she was done, she looked up. 'Any ideas?'

'It's a matter of research,' Danielle said. 'We look back. I doubt the name of the temple still exists, but the temple still should.'

Kerry nodded. She replaced the scroll in the chest and then stood up, cradling it under one arm. The others carefully replaced the floorboards until they were back to the normal and the snarling face stared upwards in its eternal sneer, glaring into darkness. Drake spoke to his team on the comms, warning that they would be coming out soon and that they had found the next scroll.

'All good up there?' he asked.

'All good,' Dahl replied. 'No activity.'

'That we can see, anyway,' Kenzie added. 'As mentioned before, there are a lot of bays on this island.'

Drake acknowledged and looked around. The team was ready to move. He led the way to the stairs and started up. Another successful find, and no sign of their enemy.

He turned aside any foul thoughts of bad guys. This was a moment for celebration. So far, the entire trip had largely been about celebration. Drake should be loving it. But he couldn't help but think, from all the successes they had had, that something was about to go terribly wrong.

CHAPTER TWENTY THREE

Drake started up the basement stairs.

His comms clicked. Dahl's voice came through. 'They're here,'

'What?'

'The enemy is here. They must have landed in one of the bays and marched to the location. They're nearer the church than we are.'

That wasn't necessarily a bad thing. Drake stopped in his tracks and held an arm up. 'Are they armed?'

'Yeah, they've all got guns. They came here to kill.'

Drake swore. 'You have the element of surprise.'

'I know it. Sit tight. We'll deal with them.'

Drake decided they would go up into the church and see what they could see. It wouldn't do them any good being cornered in a basement. He turned to the others.

'Stay calm,' he said. 'But stay together and behind us. The enemy has found the church too and is armed. My team is taking care of them now.'

He reached the church and went over to a cracked stained glass window, looked outside. All he could see was greenery – trees and brushes and the flat area surrounding the church. Anyone approaching would be easily visible. So far, there was no sign of activity.

He wondered how Dahl and the others were faring outside.

Dahl crawled through the undergrowth. The enemy were twelve strong and strung out. They were moving slowly as they neared the church, still heading uphill. Through the comms, he had determined that the rest of the Ghost Squadron were also converging on the enemy. They were creeping through the trees, through the bushes, through the scrub and the vegetation. It was a silent pincer movement, and the enemy had no idea.

Dahl crept on his elbows and knees. The slow-moving man, his quarry, slowed even more as he neared the top of the hill. He appeared to be trained, but not too well, as if he'd started military training and then quit. He held an old M16 in one hand, its barrel pointed at the floor. Dahl could tell by the way he held it he was competent, but lax.

He was so close now he could reach out and touch the guy's ankle. He breathed deeply, readying himself. One more creep forward, one last check to make sure his colleagues weren't too close, and then Dahl rose like a demon from hell, standing and looping a big arm around the man's neck. The other arm negated the gun as the struggle began.

The man bucked and reared and tried to throw Dahl off. The Swede held on implacably, all the while choking his opponent out. He didn't move, just planted his legs and fought, using his strength to keep the man in place and hold on to his gun arm. Bit by bit, the man's struggles grew weaker, and then he was hanging limp in Dahl's arms. Dahl carefully laid him on the ground and then checked for weapons. The M16 he already had, but found a knife in the guy's waistband. He took that too, wishing he had a way of tying him up and fully negating him from the fight. Never mind. This would have to do.

He jumped on the comms. 'How we doing?'

'Missed my chance,' Hayden said. 'Guy moved off too fast.'

'I got one,' Kenzie replied. 'Just disarming him now.'

'Can't act now,' Alicia said. 'Mine just met up with a friend. I could get them, but it'd get real noisy.'

'That may have to be,' Dahl hefted the M16. 'That leaves ten against us four. It's not good odds. Stay in place as they approach. Maybe you'll get your chance.'

Alicia confirmed, and the comms went silent. Dahl stayed in place. He could see another enemy ahead, but the man was too close to a colleague. They had to keep this quiet for now. There was a crackle, and then Alicia was back on the comms.

'I got one,' she said. 'Lucky, but sweet as a nut in the end.'

Dahl grinned. The odds were getting better. He moved closer to the next man, saw his colleague move ahead. There was just enough space to...

He heard a branch snap. Another man had come out of the brush and now passed Dahl on the left, walking fast. He must have stopped for some reason, and they'd passed him by. Luckily, he hadn't seen them. Dahl paused, not moving a muscle.

The enemy had now reached the top of the hill and were all stood, staring at the church. They had raised their guns. Dahl knew there were a lot of innocent people inside, many non-combatants that were all under the care of Spear Solutions. He wouldn't let these men bring their guns to bear.

From his position, Dahl saw Kenzie rise swiftly from the ground and take out another man. Instantly, though, he saw her lose her grip on the guy. He whirled and let out a shout. Everyone turned to stare.

Kenzie brought up her weapon just as Dahl did the same. They fired. In the surprise, two men went down. Alicia also opened fire, but her shot went wide. The whole area burst into commotion.

The enemy went to ground or ducked behind trees. Dahl fired again, but his bullet dug into a thick bough. The enemy fired back. The air was laced with bullets.

Dahl stayed low, crawling behind a tree. He heard the impact of a bullet, saw the foliage part to his right as another whizzed through. By his count, there were seven enemies still in action, and now they were firmly hidden under cover. He watched the trees ahead, hoping for a head to stick out. When it did, he fired, just missing.

There was a lull in the firing. Dahl and his colleagues had to conserve their ammo because, if they ran out, they would face almost certain death. He wasn't inactive though, using the hiatus to crawl to another location further to the left. From here, he could almost see around his opponent's tree. He moved further, now seeing the man's back.

Dahl took aim.

The man shifted slightly, taking him out of sight.

Dahl crept even closer. 'Keep moving,' he said through the comms. 'They still have the advantage.'

And he saw, to the right, Alicia leap out of cover and dart around her enemy's cover. She grappled with him, wrenched his gun left and right, and then dragged him to the floor. In reaction to that, Dahl's own enemy moved to *his* right, trying to get a bead on Alicia. The movement put him directly in Dahl's sights.

Dahl put a bullet through his spine. The man went down hard.

Alicia fought with her opponent on the ground, pounding him with clenched fists. She struck every vulnerable part of his body, making him gasp, and then felt him go weak. She slipped his knife from his waistband and thrust it up towards his stomach, but he twisted aside at the last moment, gasping. Alicia stayed on top, pinning him down and restricting his movements. The man fought weakly, hurt. She drew the knife back and thrust again. This time, he could only get an arm in between and the knife burst through his flesh. He screamed, suddenly galvanised. She withdrew the blade and thrust again, striking his shoulder and drawing blood. The man writhed beneath her. Alicia continued to hold him in place, but stayed low, knowing she couldn't sit up. Her only cover was on the ground.

Kenzie and Hayden inched closer to their prey, taking the long route through the foliage. They were nearing the trees at the top of the hill, moving an inch at a time.

Dahl switched positions, seeking a new target. He closed in on the enemy's position. To his right, Alicia still struggled with her opponent, though her constant thrusts of the knife told him she was winning. After a while, the struggles stopped.

Another one down.

Drake came through the comms. 'How's it going out there?'

'Steady,' Dahl said. 'They haven't realised you're inside yet. Stay quiet.'

And it was right then that one of the aides inside the church couldn't take it anymore. He was terrified, shaking and sweating, and he broke down. Started sobbing and jabbering. Dahl heard it through the comms and swore. The enemy heard it through the broken windows and turned to stare at the church.

'There're some people inside,' one of them said.

'Hiding,' another said.

'Fire,' said a third.

Drake ducked as bullets smashed into the church, crashing into brickwork and breaking windows. The stained glass fell inside, littering the floor. People started screaming and throwing themselves to the ground, scrambling out of the way. He ducked and made sure he was standing behind the brick wall. Drake turned swiftly to look at the aides and the archaeologists.

They looked terrified. One aide, a tall man, was bobbing up and down as if he couldn't decide what to do. He was going to get shot. Drake scrambled over to him, grabbed him, and forced him to the floor. He knelt before a woman with wild eyes, putting his hands on her shoulders.

'You're safe in here,' he told her. 'Just stay low.'

More glass shattered, shards flying into the room. The door was battered with bullets, woodchips flaking off, forced backwards with the impacts. Bullets zinged through the air, smashing into walls and old statues. Kerry and the other archaeologists were lying flat on the floor, their eyes fixed on Drake as he moved around people, trying to reassure them.

'We have people outside,' he was saying. 'They'll take care of this.'

He hoped he was telling them the truth.

As their enemies opened fire on the church, Hayden and the others moved forward, now in full attack mode. Hayden stepped around the tree, saw she was too close to her opponent to fire her weapon, so instead smashed him across the skull with it. He staggered, his own weapon dropping to the floor. Hayden punched him in the throat, and then the eyes. He let out a gurgle. Hayden didn't let up, firing punches at his vulnerable areas until he was on his knees.

Then she brought her own gun up and shot him.

Alicia had crawled off her bloodied opponent and now rose. The man's blood had spattered her own clothes and for a moment she stared, wondering if any of it was hers. But she couldn't feel any wounds and couldn't recall him striking her with anything other than a fist. She was fine. She crept through the undergrowth, coming up behind a new opponent.

Just as he turned away from the church.

They came face to face. The man swung his gun around. Alicia stepped in close so that he couldn't use it, then used her knife. She punched it up through his stomach all the way to the hilt, burying it. The man jerked, eyes going wide. Then he lost all his motor functions and slumped to the ground.

There were still three enemy combatants in play, and they were all firing on the church.

CHAPTER TWENTY FOUR

Drake crawled between screaming men and women.

He could tell that the volume of fire had lessened. His keen ear guessed that there were now three enemy shooters out there. Not so long ago, there had been considerably more. Even so, bullets smashed the windows and thudded into the brickwork and pounded the door. Staying low, they were fine, but panic was making some aides want to flee.

And that meant standing up.

One man with a white face and terrified eyes just shot straight to his feet and tried to run. Drake tackled him around the knees, forcing him to the floor before a bullet could catch him. The man fell hard, and Drake held on to him, shouting at him to lie still. It took several attempts, but eventually the guy quieted, though he still looked terror-stricken. Drake held onto him for several moments before trusting he could let him go. Another, a woman, also tried to stand up in panic as bullets strafed the room. A round scored her right thigh, ripping her skirt and drawing blood, and she sank to her knees. Drake pulled her to the floor and ordered her to lie still.

He crawled away, watching the rest of the aides for signs of panic.

* * *

Dahl watched as the remaining three enemy soldiers decided what to do. They were currently fairly well dug in behind their trees and vigilant, watching both sides for danger, but determined to cause terror to those caught inside the church.

Dahl heard a shout. 'Carlos, should we storm the church? We can do it, and the boss wants action.'

The man called Carlos called back, 'Do it.'

Almost immediately, the trio ran from cover, guns blazing. The rounds tore into the sides of the church, smashed through glass and wood, and imploded in the brickwork. The sound was enormous, shattering the day. Bullets rifled the air, crashing into the church's already feeble construction. Dahl saw the entire structure sway, as if it were drunk. He saw the foundations wobble and jumped right on to the comms.

'That place is weaker than we thought. The gunfire is weakening it. You have to get everyone the hell out.'

'Our enemy is shooting the shit out of it. You want us to run straight into that?' Drake responded.

'It's either that or you get crushed to death,' Dahl said. 'You choose.'

Drake cursed. He swung around, glimpsed the ceiling above, which was indeed swaying. 'We gotta leave, folks.'

They all stared at him as if he were mad. 'They're *shooting,*' Kerry said.

'And this place is about to collapse. You risk a bullet or you die under tonnes of brickwork. That's the choice.'

'You are supposed to *protect* us,' James said.

'And that's what I'm doing. I'm telling you to get the fuck out of this church.'

His words spurred them on. They ran low, keeping their heads down as bullets continued to strafe the surrounding spaces. They ran for the front door, and Mai was at the head of the pack.

She threw open the door and ran outside. A bullet flew close, but she ran on unscathed. She was out in the open now, and able to take in the entire scenario.

It all unfolded in split seconds. The enemy, three of them, were racing towards the church, guns firing. Her team were steps behind, bursting from the trees, their weapons out. Mai was metres away from the enemy leader. Through the comms she had heard his name – Carlos – and he looked the most dangerous. She filled his line of sight, put herself in harm's way, and watched as his finger tightened on the trigger.

She dodged just as he fired, and the shots went wide by inches. He didn't stop or slow down, just came on. She flung herself through the air, striking him with her body like a bowling ball hits a set of pins. She crashed to the ground. Carlos went down to his knees and lost hold of his guns.

Mai was confident, incredibly quick, and spun on the ground, kicking out. She simultaneously kicked his gun away and struck his sternum, making him cry out. He wallowed in the grass. Mai spun again almost instantaneously, sending a boot to his throat and another to his temple. Carlos double over on the grass, choking.

Mai was up in a second, but she stayed low. Two of the bad guys were still shooting, focused on damaging the church and all who were inside. The occupants were filing through the door, staying low as the entire structure shifted behind them. Drake was the last man out, the lintel above him moving from side to side.

In that split second, Dahl was following one man, Alicia another. They had their enemies lined up in their sights. Loaded moments passed. Many bullets crashed into the church. The aides and archaeologists ran towards one danger to escape another, screaming.

Drake dropped to the ground, hoping everyone else did the same. Bullets riddled the space above their heads. The church groaned as it weakened, swaying from side to side. There was a moment of pause, when the church held on and the team dived to freedom, and then the entire brick structure collapsed into itself, solid walls giving way. There was an explosion of sound and dirt, and mushroom clouds of dust and mortar rushed skywards, ballooning upwards. Glass shattered and brickwork crumbled, tonnes of debris disintegrated to the hard ground. The sound of falling rubble overwhelmed Drake's eardrums. He couldn't move, couldn't speak. Metres away, the wreckage was smashing loudly into the ground.

At the same time, Dahl and Alicia opened fire. Their bullets struck true, felling the two enemy soldiers, who went sprawling. Dahl and Alicia dived to the ground too, covering their heads.

Amidst the incredible chaos, Mai was still

fighting. She jabbed Carlos in the face, spun and kicked him in the groin. Clouds of dust spiralled out towards her, bits of debris struck her in the face. She struck again and again, driving Carlos to the floor. A chunk of wreckage landed close to them both, thudding into the grass. Mai jumped on Carlos and smashed her fingers down at his unprotected throat, making him gargle. His hands came up, but he was no match for her. She struck him without obstruction.

Soon, Carlos lay dead.

Mai rolled off him. Still, the remains of the church rolled and fell to her left. Clouds of dust enveloped her and Drake and the others. The sound echoed around the clearing. And then, suddenly, all was still.

The survivors looked up hesitantly, coughing and staring from side to side. The aides were unscathed, the archaeologists all okay. Mai climbed to her feet just as Drake stood up and took a look around.

'We all good?' he asked.

The answers came back in the affirmative, but Dahl told him he'd only knocked a couple of the bad guys out. The Ghost Squadron wouldn't resort to killing unconscious men. They got the treasure hunting team together and started to head back down to the boat. It was a long hike, but they were all hyped and determined to make it.

They had survived the cruel day. Now it was time to take the next step.

CHAPTER TWENTY FIVE

Javier was cooking under the hot sun when he got the call. Sitting up on the lounger, he snaked a hand in search of the device, picked it up and answered the call without looking at the screen.

'Carlos?' he said. 'Give me good news.'

'Umm, this isn't Carlos. It's Albert, sir.'

Albert? Who the hell was Albert?

Javier checked the screen, then went back to the call. 'Why are you calling me? And who are you?'

'I'm the pilot of the boat, sir. Carlos' boat. A couple of the guys came back. Everyone else is dead.'

Despite the heat, Javier suddenly went cold. 'Dead? The entire team. *My* team? Wait a minute... are you saying Carlos is dead too?'

A moment's silence as if the guy was stealing himself and then a deep breath, followed by, 'I'm afraid so. Carlos was killed in the battle.'

The news took Javier aback. Carlos was his second-in-command. Javier relied heavily on him. He actually knew things about Javier's businesses that he didn't. 'Damn, that's inconvenient,' he said. The fact that he was eventually going to kill Carlos himself was immaterial.

Javier tried to quell the rising tumult in his mind.

He needed a solution, and he needed it quickly.

'You say two of my team survived? How did they survive?' He asked the questions mostly to give himself time to think.

'They got knocked out early on. The other team let them live.'

'Other team? Who the hell are these guys?'

'Don't know, sir. The survivors saw very little and were overwhelmed quickly.'

Javier didn't like the sound of that. He wiped his brow, now sweating in the heat. There were others around the pool, two women in bikinis and two men sitting at the side of the pool, but Javier saw none of them. This Hellhound project was turning into a major headache.

What to do next?

He sat there and thought about it, let the pilot ramble on a bit.

'There is only one solution,' he said after a while.

'There is?'

'Yes. Only *I* can resolve this problem. Only I can bring us victory. Do you have the next clue?'

The pilot confirmed they didn't.

Then, Javier would have to ring the mole in the group. The mole had done well so far. He would continue to prove useful. Javier told the pilot to get back to the compound along with the survivors and ended the call. He would deal with the survivors later, and in a harsh way. Men working for Javier did not get 'overwhelmed.'

He made another call. Waited. It took a minute, but soon Lee's voice filled the speaker.

'Can you talk?' Javier said.

'I have a few minutes.'

'What the hell happened at the church?'

'It was crazy. A full on battle with bullets flying everywhere. The church collapsed. But the Ghost Squadron protected us all.'

'The Ghost Squadron?'

'That's what they call themselves. The protection detail hired by Kerry. There are seven of them, and they are very good.'

Javier didn't want to hear that. He swallowed. 'Did you see Carlos die?'

'Yes. The Japanese woman, Mai, took him out with ease. She just destroyed him.'

Javier could barely compute such a scenario. Carlos had been an outstanding warrior. He bit his bottom lip. 'Are they really that good?'

'The best at what they do.'

That changed things a little. Javier was going to need some expert help, it seemed. 'Do you have the next clue?'

'I have it right here. *In Singapura is the ancient ceremonial temple called Pulau Ujong. In the eastern wall find the symbol and the chest.*'

Javier wrote it down. So far, Carlos had dealt with all the machinations of the treasure hunt. Now he was going to have to step up. Not only that, but he was going to have to lead the group. And lead the attack.

Was it all worth it?

Javier thought so. The treasure in this so-called Underworld place could be vast and extremely valuable. It was worth the risk and the effort.

'I will lead the next group,' he told Lee.

'I would bring your best people.'

Lee's words struck a chord in Javier's mind. He had been thinking of doing just that, rounding up the best trained warriors in all his businesses and organising them to meet somewhere. But there was another option.

'Keep up the good work,' he said, and then signed off. He put the phone down and sat on the end of the lounger for a while, contemplating.

Could he do it? *Should* he do it?

He knew an extremely nasty group of eight men who called themselves the Malacca. They had worked for him before, entirely successfully. They too were the best at what they did and what they did was kill people. Javier could hire the Malacca to be his own set of bodyguards. That would even things up a bit.

Plus, they owed him.

Javier had given them work when they were just starting up. He had given them good word of mouth. And they knew it. They would work for him. Javier scooped up his phone again and made another call.

The Malacca would kill this Ghost Squadron. He needed the archaeologists alive to keep up the quest. Anyone else... they were dead meat.

CHAPTER TWENTY SIX

Their boat lay at anchor just off the island. The sun was just starting to go down, coalescing into an orb of slowly spreading fire. The waters were calm, smooth, gently rolling. The boat itself was raucous as the occupants described their day.

Drake had left Kenzie and Dahl on watch and had headed into the main cabin to find out what was going on. Most of the archaeologists and their aides were eating and drinking and chatting, some going over the long day, others clearly trying to forget it. Many had glasses of wine or something stronger as they contemplated how close they had come to death.

Drake saw his team mates dotted around the room. Alicia was leaning in one corner, studying the aides as if looking for someone. Hayden and Kinimaka were seated together and hunched over a plate of food. Mai was standing by the sink, drinking a glass of water. She had food in her hand. Drake drifted over to her.

'Another successful day,' he said. 'But it got a bit hairy out there.'

'If they'd been any good, they'd have won,' Mai said. 'They had all the advantage.'

Drake nodded. 'Thank God they weren't trained. We could have been trapped in that collapsing church.'

Mai took a bite of her sandwich. 'And we're one step closer to the treasure.'

Drake turned to find Kerry. The lead archaeologist was seated around the table, a copy of the latest clue in front of her. Her fellow team mates, Danielle and James, sat to either side. Drake noticed one aide, named Lee, hovered very close to the archaeologists, listening to their conversation whilst the others were scattered on all sides of the room, as if not wanting to be too close to what they considered the danger magnets. It was a way of processing their trauma.

And Drake had no doubt some of these people were suffering trauma after today. He was surprised some hadn't announced they were quitting.

Kerry was eating and drinking wine, but her attention was focused on the sheet of paper in front of her. Drake could hear Danielle talking about the next clue. The three archaeologists were absorbed.

Drake went to sit on the other side of the table. He caught Kerry's eye. 'How's it going?'

'We're starting off with the obvious,' Kerry said. '*Singapura*. Now, it sounds pretty straightforward, but you leave nothing to chance in this game. And you don't act until you're beyond sure. At least, I don't.'

'Singapura?' Drake repeated. 'Is Singapore?'

'Yes, it's the ancient name for Singapore. We've all researched it,' Kerry pulled her laptop closer. 'And we all agree. Now, the next step is to find the temple *Pulau Ujong*, but unfortunately, that doesn't exist.'

'Of course,' Drake said. 'It couldn't be that easy.'

'We're still checking,' Danielle said.

Drake left them to it. He grabbed some food of his own, poured a glass of wine, and went over to Alicia in the corner. 'You okay?'

'Not everyone here is who they claim to be,' she said.

Drake raised an eyebrow, but knew exactly what she meant. 'I agree. We have a mole. Someone who keeps passing the clue onto these bad guys. Have you figured out who it is?'

Alicia shook her head. 'Could be any one of them. Even an archaeologist. There's no way of telling.'

Drake took a bite of his sandwich. 'So, presumably, they already have the next clue and are working it out right now. Therefore, we can expect company in Singapore.'

'If they have any men left,' Alicia said with a smile.

'And if they can solve the clue,' Drake said. 'Our archaeologists are struggling.'

'That's a first.'

Drake agreed it was. He stood with Alicia for a while, enjoying her company before drifting back to the table. It was pitch black outside now; the darkness pressing right up against the windows. The boat barely moved. Inside, the aides all talked loudly, their conversations fuelled by alcohol and repressed fear. For Drake, whilst not normal, today was nothing he hadn't experienced before. For them, it must have been terrifying.

The three archaeologists were engrossed in their research, all staring at laptops. Danielle spoke as she worked.

'There's more than one way to find a temple,' she said.

'We know the Cerberim existed in the eighteenth century,' Kerry said.

'Thian Hock Keng, also known as Tianfu,' James said, tapping away. 'Is the oldest and most important temple of the Hokkien people in the country. But no,' he sighed. 'It was built in the nineteenth century.'

'There can't be that many,' Kerry mused.

'I'm still looking for one,' Danielle said.

Drake leaned forward. 'What are you gonna do if there isn't one?'

Kerry blinked at him. 'There has to be.'

Drake shrugged. 'Maybe it's been razed, knocked down, built on. Maybe it's just not there anymore.'

'Stop being practical,' Kerry said. 'This is a treasure hunt. Our landmarks *will* be there.'

Drake knew she was talking half tongue-in-cheek. He smiled and watched them work. They worked well together, each of them checking different temples.

'Oh, my God,' Danielle finally said. 'I think I have one.'

Everyone looked over at her. She tapped her screen. 'Right here,' she said. 'It's called the Temple of the Sun and Moon and, yes, it was built in the eighteenth century and is a popular tourist attraction. Open daily.'

'Great find,' Kerry said. 'But let's keep looking. There could be more.'

Drake left them to it, but after another hour Kerry finally declared that there were no more temples to look for. She was satisfied. The archaeologists sat back and took a celebratory drink.

'Tell the captain to set a course for Singapore,' Kerry said with a grin.

CHAPTER TWENTY SEVEN

Singapore was a popular tourist destination, resplendent with glittering skyscrapers and modern living. It boasted a diverse population and a tropical climate and a moral standard of living. Like anywhere, Singapore had its dismal places, but, on the surface at least, it was a beacon of good living.

Drake held the boat's front rail as they sailed into a harbour. The waters were choppy here, the boat rolling and making his stomach churn. Soon, though, the vessel had entered the harbour and calmer waters and started sailing smoothly towards the dock. Drake saw a long concrete finger, already populated by boats and, beyond it, Singapore itself jutting up to the skies. It was a large, shiny, intimidating city. People swarmed around the dock and cars drove slowly along a far road. Drake's first impression was that Singapore didn't have a lot of room.

The boat docked, and the captain declared they were safe to disembark. Kerry led the way, and since there were fifteen of them, found three taxis and made sure everyone had the right address for the Temple of the Sun and Moon. Hayden and Kinimaka appointed themselves as immediate lookouts, scouring the dock for threats and finding nothing. Then, the Ghost Squadron divided themselves up between the three cars, providing protection for everyone.

Drake ended up with Alicia and Mai in the first car. The driver told them the journey would take about an hour and that they should relax, take in the sights. The traffic would be heavy. With that, he proceeded to take them from traffic jam to traffic jam, following a sat nav route. The pavements were thronged with people of every nationality, locals and tourists alike. The shops were colourful and bright; the restaurants offering all kinds of food.

Drake spent the journey mostly in silence. The team hadn't brought any weapons to Singapore. They didn't want to get arrested or deported. The mission was very much under the radar. It was how Kerry wanted it. Of course, there was no telling where the Underworld was, what country it was in. Kerry hoped to determine that before she told anyone what they were doing.

The hour passed slowly, and then the taxi was pulling to the side of the road. The driver pointed the temple out. Drake climbed out of the car and saw the other two vehicles pulling up behind. Soon, the entire group was reunited, standing on the pavement close to the Temple of the Sun and Moon.

The temple was built of stone, timber and tiles and was of Chinese design. It comprised four halls of single storey beam frame structures. Brackets supported curved roofs. Drake saw coloured tiles, peacocks and dragons decorating the sides of the entrance hall and the roofs. He saw stone lions and gilded beams, and he wasn't even at the main door yet.

The doors stood open, admitting tourists left and right.

Drake gathered his team together. 'I think four outside and three in,' he said. 'You know what to do.' The last thing he needed to do was explain. Dahl, Kenzie, Hayden and Kinimaka volunteered to stay outside and keep a watch. Drake, Alicia and Mai were going in.

Kerry turned to her companions. 'We're looking for the eastern wall. A symbol. Probably another carving. Don't compromise yourselves, don't stand out. Don't get caught doing something you shouldn't. If you find anything, come and get me.'

There were several nods, and then the entire team started through the main entrance. Drake found himself inside an airy, colourful room filled with statues and figures and motifs that symbolised good luck. He counted about ten people in this first room and studied them all. Alicia and Mai moved off through the crowd, watching everyone. There was no sign of their enemies.

Kerry led them to the eastern wall of the first room. The team spread out and started studying the wall closely. Drake was pleased to see they took their jobs seriously, but didn't look too odd. Pretending to be tourists, they blended in well.

The search began. Drake used the comms to contact Dahl and the others outside.

'We're good in here,' he said. 'They've started searching and we're all clear.'

'Same out here,' the Swede replied. 'We've spread

out and are covering both main entrances. I guess we can see eighty per cent of the people going in or out. Can't do anything about the other twenty per cent.'

'Keep your eyes peeled, mate.'

'Always.'

Hayden and Kinimaka checked in, and then Kenzie. Drake watched the flow of humanity through the temple. There were many people and nationalities, most of them carrying rucksacks and cameras. Those wearing hats he viewed carefully, in case they were hiding anything. Drake believed he would spot a soldier amongst the crowd if there was one, a bad guy. They all had a certain look about them.

The eastern wall of the main entrance hall was combed carefully. The team spent their time and went over it twice. After a while, Kerry was confident they would find nothing. 'Three rooms to go,' she said.

'Don't forget there's a pagoda on each side,' Drake said. 'They'll also have an eastern wall.'

'Good point. We'll check that out too.'

They exited the room and walked straight into another, found the eastern wall and re-started their search. Drake, Alicia and Mai stood guard, studying the crowds whilst pretending to be tourists. So far, they'd only seen one monk wandering through and he had kept his head down, not interested in the tourists.

Drake watched the archaeologists work. They started at the bottom of the wall, all spaced out, and worked their way to the top. It was careful, painstaking work. They didn't get on their hands and knees because that would draw attention, but they did as much as they possibly could without looking too obvious. It was enough. They could inspect every inch of the wall.

Time passed. The second room was checked and yielded nothing. Drake knew there were four halls in total, plus the pagodas. The entire team moved on to the third room. Again, they took their positions and started the search. Drake looked on, still watching every face, every tourist that wandered through. Alicia and Mai did the same in other corners of the room. It was a tense, anxious time. The archaeologists were clearly worried about being caught, about attracting attention. Drake and his team were worried about far worse, the reappearance of the bad guys. Some time passed as the eastern wall was checked for any kind of symbol.

In the end, though, it revealed nothing. Kerry now looked decidedly nervous. They would be on to their last full wall. The entire team trooped through to the fourth and final room. In here, it was busy. They couldn't even see the wall at first and had to wait for the place to empty out a bit.

Eventually, though, they restarted their search. Drake again contacted Dahl and the others and was told all was okay. Inside, the aides were sweating and now on their knees. The archaeologists were clearly concerned. It wasn't going well. Already, they were about halfway across the wall and still hadn't found anything. Dake wondered briefly if they were even in the right temple.

They had to be.

He waited impatiently for the symbol to be found,

glad that Alicia and Mai were with him, glad that Dahl and the others were watching the outside. It was as safe as he was ever going to get.

CHAPTER TWENTY EIGHT

The eight members of the Malacca threaded through the crowd like ghosts.

They were the best at what they did, eight consummate killers. They could hide in crowds, drift right past people who were on lookout, and spot those people with ease. Castillo, their leader, had already passed the big blonde lookout twice, once in front and once behind, and the man had not spotted him. Castillo's companions had also reported the presence of three more observers scanning the crowds. They were reported as being good at their jobs but not in the same league as the ninja-like Malacca.

Eight killers. They had orders from Javier. Kill what he called the Ghost Squadron – the protectors – kill the aides and bring the archaeologists to him alive. All three of them. In the middle of Singapore, around this temple, that was going to be hard.

But the Malacca was the best. Castillo had completed several tough tasks with his band of Malacca. The best, for him, was a job in London where they had been assigned the job of making sure a politician died. The twist was, the old man had to look like he died of natural causes. Castillo had put a lot of thought into that one, finally coming up with the idea of a house fire in which others had died too, further clouding the fact that the politician had been murdered. In addition, the client had wanted the politician to *know* what was happening in his last moments. Castillo had facilitated that too, explaining it to him as he gave him an undetectable drug. His seven companions were all there too, carrying out their tasks to perfection. Castillo had never known such a capable band of men.

He thought about the London job now as he melted through the crowd. He could see the other three watchers from a certain angle, see them keeping an eye out for Javier's mercenaries. They expected weaker opponents. They didn't expect the Malacca.

Javier was paying very well for the service, and Castillo had a reputation to preserve. Javier wanted most of these people dead, and he wanted it to happen right away. The Malacca would have to be swift and precise and careful, and they would also have to look out for the police. They had already committed the maze of surrounding streets to memory. They knew all the best escape routes and had numerous vehicles waiting too, with drivers prepared. Castillo expected casualties, and it saddened him. Some of these men had been with him for years, one of them a decade. They had committed many murderous deeds together.

Castillo had a comms system. 'Four guards outside. That should leave three inside. Do you see them?'

Four Malacca had drifted into the church among the crowd. One of them came back now. 'Three guards inside, two women and one man. Keeping watch. They're good, but we're better. The archaeologists and their helpers are searching a wall.'

Castillo only had a rough idea of what they were searching for and didn't care. He cleared his throat. 'How close can you get?'

'Not close enough for a quick kill,' came the reply. 'This will be loud and messy. We'll have to move fast.'

It was what they were good at. Castillo had no major concerns. He watched the broad blonde man. 'Each of you choose a target. There are seven guards, eight of us. The spare man can start killing the aides. Are you all ready?'

Affirmations came through the comms. Castillo counted eight of them. The Malacca killers were ready. He was about to give the go when his comms burst into life.

'Wait,' a man said. 'There's suddenly a lot of activity. They're all moving about, including the guards. I think they've found something.'

Castillo's eyes narrowed. 'They've found what they're looking for?'

'I think so.'

He wondered what that might mean, how it would affect his team. It might mean movement on the part of the Ghost Squadron. He could still order the attack right now, but it was probably best to observe a bit more.

'Stand down,' he said. 'Wait for my order.'

He drifted away so as not to look suspicious. The trick of the Malacca was always to be moving at the same time as the crowd, always be on some person's shoulder, always having your head down and watching through your peripheries. It was an art, a lost art. Castillo felt proud that he taught it.

Now, though, he needed information. He turned again to the comms. 'Watch everything that happens. I need regular updates. If they stop moving again, I want to know about it.'

Another confirmation. Castillo cursed his bad luck. If they had moved just a few minutes previous... but he shook his head. He told his men to back off for now. The outside watchers weren't going anywhere, and he didn't want the Malacca to be noticed.

Castillo tried to let the tension slough away. It wasn't like him to get tense, but the situation was fluid and dangerous and about to become very violent. The public venue didn't sit right with him, either. He would far rather conduct a stealthy operation by night or plan a house fire, as he had done in London.

'It's all very odd in here,' his companion inside updated him through the comms. 'They had a sudden coming together, a long chat, and now they're all together looking for something. Some are standing around so people can't see what the others are doing. The guards are helping, and very watchful. I'll stay on lookout.'

'Just be careful they don't see you,' Castillo said unnecessarily. He had complete faith in his men.

A time of stasis passed. Castillo bided his time, receiving regular updates and deciding to wait, and then to wait some more. The other team was living on borrowed time. Half of them could be dead by now, and they didn't even know it.

Castillo was ready at a moment's notice. Any second now, and he would tell his team to attack.

CHAPTER TWENTY NINE

Drake was staring right at the aide who discovered the symbol as he found it.

He blinked. The mostly stationary man was suddenly jumping up and down and then trying to calm himself. He put a hand in his mouth to stop from crying out. The other aides were staring at him, and then Kerry noticed too.

She sidled up to him, looked to where he was pointing. Drake squinted. Something had them interested. His curiosity won, and he wandered over, trying to make out the object of interest.

It stood out above a niche in the wall. It was a snarling animal face, similar to a wolf. The thing had slitted eyes and fangs and was drooling. It had faded with time and was hard to spot among other carvings and etchings, but once you spotted it, you couldn't miss it.

Drake noted how it was perfectly positioned in the centre of the niche.

He glanced at the floor. It wasn't concrete; it was floorboards. The aides and archaeologists were still talking animatedly and excitedly and hadn't yet had time to check. Drake made sure Alicia and Mai were on watch and then moved to Kerry's side.

'The floor there is made of wood.'

Kerry looked down. 'You're right. We need to pull it up.' She turned to an aide. 'Do you have the crowbar?'

He nodded. Drake made a point of looking around the room. 'With all these people around? You're gonna get arrested.'

'Not if we all help,' Kerry said. 'I'll do the hard work. Everyone else shield me.'

Drake frowned. There were enough of them to easily shield Kerry if she squeezed into the niche and got down on her knees. The aides alone could do it. He watched as Kerry sank to her knees and then the aides all stood with their backs to her, ranged around. Alicia came over to lend a hand. Drake prayed Kerry would work quick.

Whatever noise she made was masked by the hubbub within the room. A group of tourists drifted through, walking right past the aides without noticing anything amiss. Drake continued to watch them all. Minutes passed. The room grew hotter, at least for Drake. He was starting to sweat.

Right then, he saw Kerry get to her feet. It looked like she was holding something in her arms. She said something to the surrounding aides he didn't catch but, all of a sudden, they parted ranks.

Now Drake saw Kerry holding the familiar chest in both hands. It was dusty and dirty, but he could see the usual hideous faces and scenes. Kerry held it to her chest. She was grinning. Within seconds, she was across to him.

'We have to take this somewhere quieter to read the clue. We can't do it in here.'

Drake agreed. From his position, he had a good view of the eastern pagoda. The place was empty. 'How about we take it in there?'

Kerry looked over. At first she looked reluctant, maybe thinking the place could get busy, but then she nodded.

They moved off. Drake checked the floorboards and saw she'd replaced them just right. The entire team filed out of the fourth room and entered the pagoda. As he'd noticed, it was currently empty.

Apart from them.

Kerry placed the chest on the ground and knelt before it. The other archaeologists and aides crowded around her. Alicia and Mai guarded the doorway.

'Make it quick,' Alicia said.

Kerry wasn't drawing it out. She unhooked the clasps that held the chest together and then lifted the lid. Drake saw another yellowed scroll, neatly rolled. It looked like they were still on the right trail.

Kerry reached in and plucked out the scroll. She unrolled it and briefly read what was on the page.

'What does it say?' an aide, Lee, asked.

Kerry opened her mouth to speak, but right then Alicia appeared. She stood right in front of the chest, towering over Kerry. 'I think that's a mistake,' she said.

Kerry looked up at her. 'What?'

'I said I think you're making a mistake. All along, the bad guys have found us, found the location. How is that possible?'

Kerry pursed her lips. 'It's right here. Everyone's seen it anyway. What do you want me to do?'

'Confine your reading to just a few people, not everyone.'

The aides and the other two archaeologists were all now staring at Alicia as if she'd lost her mind. Most of them looked affronted. Danielle, though, was nodding.

'She may have a point.'

Kerry frowned. 'I think you're out of line. You're calling one of these people a traitor. And with no proof. And you-' she looked at Danielle. 'These are your friends.'

'Not all of them,' Danielle said with a touch of exasperation.

'I thought... oh, it doesn't matter what I thought. We're a team. We should act as one.' And with no more comment, she read out the clue.

'*A sea journey to the great volcano on the Islands of Solomon. Go to the eastmost narrowest cave and you will find the chest in its depths.*'

The entire team took it in silently. Some were still glaring at Alicia. Others stared at the scroll. Danielle and James sank down beside Kerry, reading over her shoulder.

'A great volcano,' James mused. 'Interesting.'

Kerry replaced the scroll in the chest. 'I won't replace it for fear of being caught. We'll deal with that issue at a later date. Now all we have to do is get out of here.'

That was where Drake came in. He jumped on the comms. 'About to exit,' he said. 'Get ready for us.'

'Understood,' Hayden said. 'We're good out here.'

Drake walked over to Kerry. 'Stay among your aides. Hide the chest as well as you can. Once we're out in the street, we're clear all the way to the boat.'

Kerry nodded. She rose, hugged the chest tight

under her right arm. The aides crowded around her. Drake looked around and then abruptly stopped. He thought he'd seen a face in the crowd, one he'd seen before, but almost immediately the face had vanished. Now there were just hunched shoulders and stiff spines where he was looking. It was an odd moment. For a while now, he'd felt slightly threatened, as if someone was observing him from a mile off, unobserved themselves. It set the nerves jangling down his spine. But he knew that couldn't be right. Apart from the fact that they were inside a room, he had seen no one who might stand out.

He checked on the comms again. 'Just be careful,' he said. 'I thought I saw someone just now who was hanging around before. Didn't catch my eye, but looked familiar. Just a heads up.'

'Got it,' Dahl said. 'I'm all clear.'

The others all chimed in, too. Everything seemed fine. Drake continued at Kerry's side, keeping her hidden in the crowd. They crossed the fourth room and entered the third. A monk now stood in the far corner, observing people and smiling and nodding. Drake silently cursed their luck. That was all they needed. Steadily, they wandered unhurriedly across the room, concealing Kerry as best they could. They didn't stop to look at anything on the way, but then they did appear to be on their way out.

Drake watched everyone, including the monk. It was a fraught passage, but eventually they made it to the second room. In here, it was thick with people, and the group had to separate to thread their way through. Drake leaned into Kerry, helping to screen the chest with his own body as he draped an arm over her shoulders and smiled. Just another happy couple.

Too slowly, they crossed the room.

It was then that Kinimaka came on the comms. 'Hey, heads up. I think we're being watched.'

Drake coughed to hide the movement of his lips. 'What? Why?'

'I have a bad feeling, but it's not just that. Not just instinct. I saw a guy about a half hour ago winding his way through the crowd. For a millisecond our eyes locked, then he was gone. I've just seen him again.'

'Same position?'

'Just about.'

'Anyone else feeling bad about this?' Drake asked.

Nobody else had seen anything amiss.

'If we're being watched, they're damn good,' Dahl said.

'Be on high alert,' Drake said. 'We're in the second room and about to make our way through the first. We should be out in minutes.'

And that was when the Malacca attacked.

CHAPTER THIRTY

Drake saw his man coming in from the right, past the priest. His face looked like it had been carved in stone and bore a terrible expression. The man was a killer, through and through, and the way he moved made him look intensely capable. He slid through the crowd as if they weren't there and, as he moved, Drake saw a long, sharp stiletto blade drop into his hands.

They were here to make a swift kill.

He had no time to warn anyone, no time to prepare. He met his would-be killer in front of the priest and reached down for the wrist that held the stiletto. When he did, the man head-butted him and thrust his free fist at Drake's ribs. Drake twisted out of the way of both strikes.

Elsewhere. Alicia and Mai were suddenly under attack. Men came at them from different angles, men they noticed only just in time. They were in defence mode immediately, but always ready for battle.

Voices filled the comms. Dahl and Kenzie saying they were under attack. Hayden and Kinimaka warning about suspicious characters and then grunting with exertion. Drake concentrated on the man in front of him, who was a superior fighter.

The man wrenched his arm free, pivoted and thrust with the stiletto. Drake let it slide under his arm, moved in, and landed a couple of blows. The guy didn't even flinch, just withdrew the stiletto and moved aside.

Drake jabbed and moved easily. The crowd parted around the fighting men. Someone screamed. The priest stared at them in disbelief. But it wasn't just Drake's fight he was looking at. He could see Alicia and Mai battling too, violence throughout the room. He could see the archaeologists and the aides backing away into a corner, the tourists starting to run or just standing there, unsure what to do. Drake imagined the scene would be similar outside. But he had no more time to reflect, as his opponent struck again.

Dahl couldn't believe what was happening. The square outside the temple was packed with people, men and women of all ages coming and going. A long-haired, reedy man came at him fast and hard, a thin knife clasped in one hand. Dahl skipped away, almost tripping over a tourist. The man gave him an angry glare until he saw the flashing blade.

Then he ran.

Dahl struck first, smashing the man in the biceps. It was a strong lunge, and it stopped the man in his tracks, making him blink in surprise. Dahl took advantage of that fact and stepped in with an uppercut. This the man dodged, and then span on the spot, sending a kick at Dahl's head. Dahl ducked it, just in time to see the thin blade come at him again. This time, he skipped back. The blade didn't reach him. From the corner of his eye he saw the square move into chaos mode as Hayden, Kinimaka and Kenzie all started fighting. It was turning into a furious melee.

Screams and shouts rang up to the sky. Dahl had to ignore the bedlam. His opponent was good. He struck and struck again, nicking Dahl's throat with a sudden thrust. Dahl could feel the blood trickling, nothing major, but it was still a wound.

He had to get a firm hold of his opponent, deprive him of the blade. He slipped around the guy, trying every angle, but the man was aware of his every move. Blocks and thrusts and side-steps came in, and nothing changed. Dahl still faced an armed opponent. A tourist almost tripped him as he flew by, striking Dahl's heel. Dahl staggered but caught himself just as the blade thrust again, this time flashing past his skull. On the return swing the man tried to cut him, but Dahl danced away.

Hayden, Kinimaka and Kenzie all struggled against accomplished opponents. It was a hard face-off, with everyone skirting around each other, all looking for an opening. Around them, the crowd screamed and scurried.

Drake pretended to turn to the priest, trying to distract his opponent. There was a moment when the man hesitated, sent his eyes questing for the priest's position. Drake took advantage, stepping in. He dealt three instant, devastating blows, all targeted at vulnerable areas. The first was at the throat, the second the sternum and the third the groin.

None of them hit the mark.

Drake was astounded. The guy was lightning quick. Ordinarily, his blows would have ended the fight. Now the guy had an advantage, knowing he was a little bit quicker. Drake backed off as he came again. There was an exhibit to his left, a large stone plate. Drake grabbed it and threw it at the armed man, saw it glance off his forehead. This upset him and drew a little blood. He staggered. Drake took instant advantage, stepping in, but at that moment a running tourist smashed into him, unbalancing him.

Drake fell to one knee.

Both men took a few seconds to recover. Drake grabbed another item, this a pot, and threw it at the man. It was brushed aside, but still an opening was created. The stiletto was pointing at the floor.

Drake lunged without grace. It was an ungainly strike, but it finally gave him some leverage. His attack punished his opponent's midriff – one, two, three – all strikes hitting home. The man folded, and then Drake was on him, smashing down at his exposed neck. This attack sent the guy to his knees, grunting. Drake treated him to a knee in the face and then a boot to the neck. The man went down, still struggling. The stiletto fell away.

Drake knew he couldn't leave this opponent conscious. He straddled him, hooked an arm around his throat, and choked him into oblivion. It took just a few seconds and then the guy's head hit the floor.

Drake looked up. He grabbed the stiletto. The priest had fished a mobile phone from a pocket and was, presumably, not calling his grandmother. Drake saw Alicia trading blows with her short-haired opponent. This guy was much taller than her, towering over her, and looked menacing. But Alicia matched him blow for blow. Mai was darting hard and fast in a corner, using all her skills. Her opponent was good, but barely managing to keep up with her. Drake saw the man's stiletto fly away, skittering across the floor. Then Mai span three times, each time catching the guy with a kick to the head. At the end, he fell, landing on his knees. Mai's fourth kick almost took his head off.

They both turned to Alicia.

Drake ran and slid in, almost taking a slow tourist out in the process. He kicked Alicia's opponent in the shins, knocking him off his feet. The guy staggered in an ungainly manner, but was still lethal, holding his weapon.

Drake and Mai hit him from two sides, both targeting his ribcage. There was the satisfying sound of something snapping and then a high-pitched gasp. Alicia finished him with a punch to the side of the head.

'You're welcome,' Mai said.

'Could've finished him,' Alicia sniffed. 'Just a matter of time.'

'Which we don't have,' Drake said. 'The others are fighting outside.'

By now, the archaeologists and aides were coming out of their corner, looking scared and dazed.

Drake turned to Kerry. 'Stay here for now,' he said. 'There are others outside. We have to go help.'

'Are we safe?'

'So long as these assholes don't wake up,' Alicia kicked her opponent.

With that, the three of them started running for the exit. The priest still hadn't moved, which Drake found surreal, and was still on the phone. There was no sound of sirens, just the din of the tourists, both inside and out.

Drake led the race outside. He ran into the bright sunshine and stopped quickly, searching for his team. Dahl was on the other side of the square, faced with a strong opponent. Hayden and Kinimaka were close, struggling to stay on top of their fights. Kenzie had her man on his knees and was battering his head.

Drake jumped on the comms. 'We're here,' he said. 'Let's get rid of these guys and then get the hell out of here.'

'Easier... said... than... done...' Dahl gasped.

Drake made a beeline for him. 'Hang on, mate. I'm on my way.'

CHAPTER THIRTY ONE

The three newcomers made all the difference to the battle. Drake helped Dahl, Alicia went to Hayden, and Mai chose Kinimaka. Kenzie looked to be doing okay. Together, they hit their opponents from both sides simultaneously and made them bleed.

Around them, the square was in uproar. Some people still made their way across, oblivious. Others stood around the sides, filming on their mobile phones. And more were running away, some crying out in shock and fear. The traffic close by had long since ground to a halt, cars and trucks idling as their drivers watched the commotion.

Drake struck at the man's back, hitting kidneys hard. The man stumbled into Dahl, who grabbed him in a headlock and forced him to his knees. Drake negated the stiletto by grabbing the wrist and twisting. The man had to let it go to prevent breakage.

Dahl choked him out. The man fell, nerveless. They looked up. The others were now getting the best of their opponents. Drake noticed Kenzie had defeated hers. She was closest to the temple.

He jumped on the comms. 'Kenzie, run into the temple. Grab the archaeologists and protect them. We need to get back to the boat.'

Kenzie raced into the temple. Soon, Mai and Alicia had helped Hayden and Kinimaka finish their opponents off. Kinimaka broke his man's neck and flung him aside. Hayden kicked her man in the throat, crushing his larynx. They were both bloody and bruised and didn't want their opponents' chasing them again.

Kenzie brought the archaeologists and aides out of the temple in a tremendous rush. Eight of them, all in a group. They raced down the steps, looking about wildly. Drake raised a hand and waved at them.

'This way,' he yelled.

The entire group broke towards him. It was a sudden stream of people, all running in the same direction. Drake wondered briefly how long the men they'd choked would remain unconscious. Not long enough, he guessed.

They stuck together, a large group running from the square. Dahl led the way, Drake dropped to the back. He watched their rear more than he watched where they were going, hoping they weren't being followed. If they could just get away from the area before...

They weren't that lucky. Two assassins suddenly emerged from the temple, looking their way. Instantly, they set off in pursuit. Drake relayed the information across the comms.

'We have company,' he said. 'Eight o'clock.'

Most of the team dropped to the back of the running pack, letting Dahl lead the way back to the boat. Two enemies were chasing, and then Drake saw a third rise to his feet, cough, and take off in pursuit. The group ran along a busy street, threading through tourists, a stream of cars passing to their right. Bright and gaudy signs hung outside shops that hugged the pavement. Dahl barged people aside, barely slowing. The rest just followed in a long stream.

Drake saw their enemies were catching up. He turned a corner, then stopped and slipped down an alley. He waited, Alicia at his back. Counted the seconds. When he heard the sound of pounding feet, he stepped back out, right into the face of an assassin.

Drake backhanded him. The man ran right into it. Blood burst from his nose, splattering the ground. He reeled back, falling unconscious. Drake stepped right out, and Alicia came around him. Together, they faced the other two men.

Who struck without pause. Drake and Alicia fended them off. Drake grabbed one and threw him bodily into a wall, saw him bounce off. This man then staggered back across the pavement right back at Drake, who led with an elbow to the face. The elbow hit with blunt force, smashing a cheekbone. The man didn't flinch, just brought his arms up and struck with lightning quickness. Drake blocked the blows but stumbled backwards into the road. Luckily, the traffic was slow, and he ended up sitting on the front end of a Toyota, fists raised.

His opponent struck left and right. Drake covered up. The car was still moving, its lone occupant leaning out of a window and shouting. Drake felt himself dragged along its side. His rib struck a mirror. Drake led with an uppercut that smashed right under his aggressor's chin. The man reeled back, arms flailing. Drake pushed away from the car and led with a kick to the stomach. Again, the man staggered back. Drake followed, still kicking, and then targeted all the nerve endings, bringing the man to his knees. Now wasn't the time to hold back. These assassins needed to be taken out of the game completely.

He sent the palm of his heel smashing into the guy's nose, breaking it and sending the cartilage up towards the man's brain. It was a killing blow. The guy folded instantly. Drake turned to Alicia.

Working fast, the Englishwoman struck left and right, grabbed her opponent's head and slammed it into a window with such force the glass cracked from side to side. The man visibly shuddered, his legs turning to jelly. He slid down, but Alicia didn't stop there. She brought up her boot and kicked him in the side of the head as he slithered down the glass. Her strike closed his eyes, maybe forever. He certainly wouldn't be going anywhere soon.

Drake studied their rear. Nobody else was chasing them. The assassin herd had been thinned, it seemed.

Drake could still see Dahl at the head of the running group. They were further along the road, racing as fast as they could through the crowds. Often, they were forced into a jog and sometimes a fast walk. Drake and Alicia turned now to chase after them. They found it easier to run along the side of the road next to the kerb.

Drake ran carefully, still watching behind them. Slowly, taking their time, they caught up with the group.

Dahl's voice came through the comms. 'Just a few minutes to the harbour.'

'Any sign of the cops?' Drake asked.

'Just the sirens.'

Sirens were wailing in the air now, loud and raucous. Drake couldn't see their source but knew a large police presence was on its way, maybe even now arriving at the square. Dahl continued to cut his way through the crowd.

It was a long, hard, sweaty run. The archaeologists and aides straggled out, some slower than others. Some were labouring, falling back, others right on Dahl's heels. Drake saw the Kerry was struggling with the chest. Kinimaka ran to help her.

They ran on, crossing a wide road and causing chaos. Vehicles swerved and braked, tail lights flashing on. Horns blasted. Drake winced, knowing it would attract attention, but they just looked like a group of tourists running across a road. Or, at least, that was what he hoped.

The car drivers were angry, gesticulating. Some refused to slow, barging their way right past the pedestrians. One such man tried to drive through Dahl, but suddenly found himself staring at the big, angry Swede. Dahl stood his ground, squaring up to the car, and the driver suddenly braked. Someone without good instincts slammed into his rear end. Dahl steadily continued on.

They all reached the other side safely and started threading their way through a new crowd. The harbour was in sight. Drake craned his neck. He could see their boat. He looked around. Still no signs of pursuit nor any police vehicles. Finally, he allowed his racing mind to calm a little.

He wondered who the hell the assassins were. They certainly were a cut above the men they'd encountered so far. Had someone else sent them? How many entities were they up against?

Soon, they were alongside the boat, and then the captain was getting them moving. Before he could go one inch, Drake noticed a commotion among the aides.

'I can't do this anymore,' one man was shouting, gesturing angrily at Kerry. 'I didn't join to be attacked and beaten. It's too much.'

Drake walked towards the uproar. The entire gang of aides and archaeologists were stuck in some sort of confrontation at the back of the boat, all facing each other.

'It's the same with me,' another said, this time a woman. 'I didn't anticipate all this. I don't want to die doing my job.'

Drake could understand it. These people shouldn't have to put up with mercenaries, chases, and assassins.

Kerry was staring at them. 'I understand,' she said, still holding the chest. 'But do you really want to leave right now? In the middle of a strange city?'

The woman spoke first. 'It's better than getting attacked again. I've been paid. I can make my own way back home.'

The man looked like he agreed with her, walking across to stand beside her. They formed a lonely red-faced duo, challenging the others. Drake saw that Jed and Lee and another aide didn't seem to share their reluctance to continue. He had to remind himself that these people were civilians, unused to combat.

And, of course, they certainly hadn't signed up for it.

He moved to stand by Kerry for support.

'If you want to leave, I can't stop you,' she said. 'I wouldn't advise it just yet, though. There're enemies in this city.'

'They're not chasing us,' the woman said.

Kerry spread her arms. 'Sure,' she said unhappily. 'I don't recommend it, but sure. Leave if you want to.'

The duo didn't hesitate. Together, they both turned and walked off the boat back onto the dock. Drake stared after them, having no emotion one way or another. Yes, it was his duty to protect all these people and, so far, he thought they'd done a pretty good job. But the people were free to make up their own minds. He couldn't force them to stay. And maybe they were better off this way.

A few minutes passed. The drive enquired whether he could set sail. Kerry looked pointedly at her remaining aides.

'Anyone else want to leave?'

They all shook their heads. Drake watched them closely. All three were men, and they all worked very hard at their jobs.

'Then let's go,' Kerry said.

They sailed through the harbour, heading for deeper seas. As they went, Kerry convened a big meeting in the main cabin. When the room quietened, she recited the clue from memory.

'A sea journey to the great volcano on the Islands of Solomon. Go to the eastmost narrowest cave and you will find the chest in its depths.'

She studied the room. 'What can we make of this?'

'Well, obviously the Islands of Solomon are the Solomon Islands,' Hayden spoke up first. 'I guess we look for the biggest volcano.'

Kerry nodded. She passed instructions on to the captain. The group looked at the chest and broke out some food and drink, and then sat down. They were subdued for a while, still trying to recover from events at the temple. Nobody wanted to talk about it. Drake felt calm and relaxed and just sat back with his team, gauging the room. They seemed upset at the loss of their own teammates, some of them even angry that the pair had walked out. Kerry made only brief comment, preferring to keep most of her thoughts to herself.

Drake leaned back and looked at Hayden. 'Those guys weren't mercs,' he said. 'They were top drawer. Somebody else really wants this treasure.'

'Yeah, they're pulling out all the stops. We have to be wary of what comes next.'

Drake agreed. 'The Underworld must be something special.'

'Well, it holds all the treasure of the Cerberim, which must have been substantial.'

'I have faith in Kerry,' Drake said. 'She's good at her job.'

He turned and watched the boat cutting through the seas, already turning on its new chartered course towards the Solomon Islands. They were sailing in the wake of the Cerberim, centuries later, in search of their long-lost treasure, and he felt fully invested in the job. He would help Kerry find it, and he would keep her safe whilst she did.

It was their job.

CHAPTER THIRTY TWO

Javier took out his knife and stabbed it into the desk. It stuck quivering; the tip embedded in the wood. Javier regarded the shivering handle with fury.

'Dead? All of them?'

The man named Castillo, the leader of the Malacca, spoke with a muted fury of his own. 'They killed five in total. They escaped. The Malacca have never been bested this way.'

'Then they're good? This team of protection agents is fucking good?'

'The best I've ever seen,' Castillo said. 'I now have to restart the Malacca from scratch.'

Javier didn't feel a scrap of sympathy. The Malacca had met their match; it seemed. Their loss had put him in a far more difficult position. With no compassion, he ended the call and went back to staring at the handle of his knife.

He couldn't stay angry. He needed to think. With the Malacca out of the picture, he was back to his own men. And *me*. He had always wanted to lead this operation. Now perhaps it was time. But he couldn't just barge in there as they had been doing. He needed an angle, something different. Javier took the knife out of the desk and scraped his stubble with it, thinking.

What to do?

The answer was staring him in the face. Against him was arrayed the protection crew, the archaeologists and the aides. He was attacking them all, trying to hurt them all at the same time as wanting the archaeologists alive. Maybe, just maybe, they could abduct one of the archaeologists, take one out of the game and force them to help.

With this in mind, Javier called his remaining men together to a meeting in the garden. He joined them when they had gathered, everyone standing around a tall, white figure of an evil genie that sat in his garden. If you told everyone to meet by the genie, or the djinn, or the wraith, everyone knew where that was. Thus, it was a good place to conduct a meet.

He strode across the grass, heading there now. It wasn't far from the back door. The weather was hot and cloudless, with not a breath of wind in the air. The garden was quiet, the stillness not even broken by the gathering of his men. They were all quite subdued, knowing what had happened to the Malacca and to Carlos.

Javier made his way to the statue and climbed up onto the wide plinth. He could easily stand here and look out over his men.

'You all know about the death of Carlos, my second in command,' he said. 'Which has set me back somewhat. Carlos handled much of the everyday stuff. I have not yet appointed a new second, but it strikes me now that we may soon have a chance to do so.'

Some men, who thought they were next in line, straightened.

Javier counted them. Eighteen. All looking expectant, aware, prepared. They would all do what he wanted them to do. He looked over the assembly.

'I have many businesses,' he said. 'You all know this. I have many resources too. I do not need to follow the trail of the Cerberim. I do not need to find this Underworld. It is surely low on my list of needs. And there is much to take care of, much that demands my attention. So why chase this treasure?'

He didn't need to explain himself, but Javier felt his men needed a rallying call. They had faced loss after loss. Now they needed to feel something, something uplifting.

'We deserve it,' he said. 'We are pulling together against our losses, and we deserve this. You deserve it. We all do. What we are doing is something new. A great quest. We've never done this before. Few people have. I think giving up now, after all this, would be a massive failure. Don't you?'

His men nodded, some angrily.

'We're up against a good team, one of the best. Is that going to stop us?'

Now there were angry head shakes and several stentorian shouts of, *'No!'*

'We won't let them beat us!' There was a cheer. 'We can be the first to find this treasure. It can be ours.' Now over half his men were cheering, the others smiling or nodding their heads. He saw no gloominess among them.

'Carlos is dead, and the Malacca beaten,' he said. 'But we are still here, and *we* can win the day. Do you believe you can do this?'

Now all the men were yelling in the affirmative

and raising their fists to the air. He had them. They were ready. Javier spent a bit more time building them up and then went back to the house. It was time to make a phone call.

He dialled the number he knew from memory. When the phone was answered, he said, 'It's me.'

'Hi. I can't talk for long. My position was made harder today.'

'That's not good. How?'

'Two other aides left the crew. There're only three of us left now.'

'I see. Well, that's not too bad. Do you have the next clue?'

Lee recited it down the phone slowly as Javier wrote it all down. 'The Solomon Islands?' Javier repeated. 'And some great volcano.'

'I guess we'll know it when we get there.'

'And so will we. You have done well so far, Lee. I hope this doesn't expose you.'

'Me too. I am proving to be most helpful. It throws them off the scent.'

'Stay undercover as long as you can. And Lee... ?'

'Yes?'

'We'll see you in the Solomons.'

CHAPTER THIRTY THREE

Drake studied the Solomon Islands as they slipped by to the left. Their task wasn't an easy one. The Solomons consisted of six major islands and over 900 smaller ones, many obviously too small to be the target. It would take a while to traverse the chain.

The team took it in their stride. Kerry, Danielle, and James spent all their time out on deck, searching for the great volcano. The aides lounged inside, doing little but waiting for when they were needed. Drake and his team watched everything, from boats bobbing on the horizon to people watching from the islands. He trusted no one.

At midday there was a squall. Nothing major, but it cut the visibility, and the boat was forced to stop, to drop anchor. They couldn't afford to miss anything in the gloom. They stayed like that for two hours until the squall passed over and it became bright again. Drake had continued their watch and saw nothing sinister.

Time passed. The Solomons were spread out, and they couldn't go too fast. They didn't want to have to make this journey again in the other direction. The landscape they passed was impressive, but nothing stood out as a great volcano. Drake was hoping to see a smoking mountain, but knew the thing was probably dormant. At the least, he expected so. He did not know the names of most of the islands they passed, and neither did anyone else. Eventually, they became a blur. The archaeologists watched hungrily as each land mass crept by, comparing what they could see to knowledge they'd scoured from the internet.

Eventually, they all let out a cry.

Drake had seen it, too. A craggy little island dominated by an enormous mountain. Its black sides were steep and rocky, all the way from the base to the coned top. Drake saw a stony island made of black rock, inhospitable, barren. He wondered if they could even pick their way across it. But, then, the Cerberim had done it.

There was some argument as to whether this was the right island. James debated they hadn't yet seen them all, and he was right. Could there be another suitable candidate further on? Kerry claimed it was perfect, obvious. The entire island was mostly a volcano. Eventually, Kerry won out and James lost, but the pair were too excited to be angry with each other. They wasted no time organising the boat.

Soon, they were motoring to shore and then landing in the surf, dragging the boats to anchor. The beach could barely be called one, all rocks and boulders and a tiny patch of sand. The team gathered around as Kerry plotted a course to the east side of the volcano.

It took her minutes, and then she looked up. 'Everyone ready?'

Whilst they had been doing that, Drake and his

team had been scouting the area. Nothing looked amiss. The highest ground they could reach so far was a mini-hill a few hundred yards to the east, and it didn't provide much of a view. But Kenzie ran to it and gave the all-clear over the comms. Drake could see no imminent danger and nodded at Kerry.

'We're ready.'

They all started out, heading straight for their destination. It was rough going, the ancient lava flows providing little pathway. Drake found himself watching his footing as much as the environment, and so did the rest of the Ghost Squadron. Dahl and Kinimaka ranged further out, checking the territory. Mai watched their backs. They were ready for all dangers.

The journey was fraught with risk. One slip on this terrain and you could break an ankle with ease. They picked their way gently through the rocks, heads down. Ever so slowly, the volcano grew larger in their sights.

The sun beat down most of the morning. Occasionally a cloud drifted by, obscuring it, affording them some relief, but for the most part there was unbridled heat. Drake sweated and removed his jacket and received a whistle from Alicia, and tried to ignore her. As he walked, he reflected the team hadn't come together much in the last few days. It was an odd situation. Here they were working as one, on top of each other almost, and yet he was thinking how little they'd communicated. Well, it wasn't such a bad thing. At least they weren't getting on each other's nerves.

The journey went on. Hours passed. The lava

flows became deep, requiring some climbing out the other side. The volcano grew and grew, finally filling their sights. Kerry kept them headed east and looked with ever-increasing scrutiny for a cave entrance in the eastern flanks. She appeared anxious. In deciding this was the right volcano, she had overruled a member of her team. If they couldn't find the cave, or if it was actually the wrong one, she would be made to look incompetent.

But Kerry soldiered on, led by Drake's team. Drake and the others saw nothing dangerous on the journey. They were the only people on this island. Maybe the only living things barring insects. It was a hostile place.

It took some time, and the volcano grew larger and larger, but finally Kerry saw a cave entrance in the volcano's eastern side, arched, jagged and not too large. If you weren't looking for it, you could easily pass it by. But her eagle eyes latched on to it and she shouted out the discovery and the entire entourage stopped, aides smiling as much as the archaeologists.

'What do we have here?' James said with a grin.

Kerry now led them towards it. They stopped again right outside the cave and took a few minutes to eat and drink, get their body fuel up. They probably wouldn't want to stop inside the cave. Drake sat with Alicia and took a few moments out to talk to her.

'You enjoying our new job now it's become more interesting?'

'It's moving forward.' Alicia shaded her eyes to look at him. 'This entire process is about moving forward. So, yeah, I've come to terms with it. We're not saving the world, but maybe that's a good thing.'

'Agreed. We've saved the world as much as anyone in the past few years.'

'The only thing that worries me...' she said. 'Where are we going? None of us are getting any younger. I mean, our time doing this is limited.'

'You're worried about old age?'

'Aren't you? Once we can't physically beat our enemies anymore, what do we do then?'

'That's a long way off.'

'I know. But the question still exists.'

'You have to find the thing that satisfies you.'

'I did.' she touched his elbow. 'Didn't you know?'

He grinned. 'I meant – in life. Something that brings you contentment.'

'I know what you meant. But Drake, I've been running since I could join the army. That's been a long time. It's all I've ever known. Even being part of this team, I'm trying to move forward. Always looking for the next thing.'

'The next thing,' he said. 'Is a dodgy volcano.'

She sighed. 'But tomorrow? Next week? Next year?'

'You're very demanding,' he said also with a sigh. 'I don't know what to do with you.'

'I could think of a few things, but not here.'

'That's unlike you. You're usually ready to whip it out anywhere.'

She laughed and gave him a punch. 'Maybe I'm mellowing in my old age.'

He snorted. 'Don't even think like that,' he said. 'It's a mindset. You think you're young, you'll stay young. You think you're past it, that's when you're done.'

Alicia nodded. Right then, Kerry climbed to her feet and asked if everyone was ready. A few people took their final swigs and then the entire team was up. They faced the cave. Drake insisted his people lead the way.

This time, Hayden and Kinimaka went first. Torches out, they stepped under the cave entrance and found themselves immediately in a dark, jagged passage. The tunnel twisted and turned but didn't branch off. It was narrow enough that they had to proceed in single file. Drake didn't have to warn Hayden, in the lead, about the possibility of traps.

'Spread out,' Kerry said. 'Don't bunch together. If something happens, we might get lucky.'

Drake didn't like the sound of that. He worried Hayden was exposed, that she might miss something. Of course, he knew he shouldn't worry about his capable friend, but he couldn't help it. He worried for them all.

The tunnel led them downwards, undulating softly. Inside, it was cooler, damper. The air smelled musty. The rocky sides were hard and far from smooth. Drake found one thing amusing. Here they were, going underground, deep in the bowels of a volcano, on the quest of a lifetime, and the only thing he could smell was everyone's deodorant.

The journey went on for some time. A space opened out to the right, something deep and dark, offering an endless drop, but the pathway was quite wide and they didn't feel too anxious. Hayden stepped carefully, one foot in front of the other, checking everything carefully and hoping she didn't miss anything. It was a tense time. Drake watched her as best he could, and he kept an eye on the passage, looking for pitfalls. Who knew what the Cerberim had left behind to trap the unwary?

A while later, Hayden paused. She said, 'I thought I felt something.'

They all stopped. The air was still and quiet. Drake felt nothing. Hayden stayed in place, but then shrugged her shoulders and moved on. Kinimaka, next in line, also stopped. 'Yeah,' he said. 'Me too.'

They waited. Nothing happened. Drake said, 'What did you feel?'

'A change in air pressure. A movement. I'm not sure.'

Kerry went through next and then Lee, one of the aides. Fifth in line was a guy named Jack, the third aide. As he walked there was a sudden shift above him, a grinding sound, and something fell from the ceiling. Drake saw the movement and dived headlong away from it. The others did the same. Jack was left scrambling as something unknown fell from the roof and crashed into place on the floor. Jack screamed and there was a terrifying crunch. After that, Jack stopped screaming.

Drake whirled. He saw that some kind of metal portcullis had dropped from the roof directly on to Jack. The man had taken the full force and now, as the portcullis raised itself back up, it took his body with it, twisting it grotesquely. Jack's body rose a few feet and slipped off the rising portcullis, falling into the dark depths to the right. One minute Jack was there, the next he was gone forever.

Drake stared in disbelief. Everything had happened so suddenly. There was utter silence among the crew.

'I think I triggered the mechanism,' Hayden said softly. 'Age slowed it down. It only started working again when Jack walked underneath.'

Drake saw a low, oddly shaped stepping stone. 'That,' he said, shining the light on it. 'Look out for them from now on.'

'*Should* we continue?' Danielle asked the question.

It was a moral question. One of their party had just died. Should they really continue with the quest?

Kerry answered. 'I don't think we can quit now,' she said. 'We're too far along. And our enemies won't quit. We don't want them to get their hands on it for nefarious purposes. Jack knew the risks, and so do we. Nobody has to continue, but I think it's the right thing to do.'

The aides and the archaeologists just looked at each other, saying nothing. It might be a moral decision, but nobody wanted to give up the quest despite the danger.

'There's still a long way to go,' Kerry said. 'Shall we start?'

Drake and his team, at the same time, knew there was nothing they could have done to save Jack. He had fallen prey to a devious trap, out of the blue.

Hayden turned and started leading the way once more.

CHAPTER THIRTY FOUR

The tunnel twisted, going sometimes upward and sometimes down. It snaked and rarely ran in a straight line, cut deep through the solid rock. Its edges were treacherous and the void to their right came and went. In front, Hayden watched her step, backed closely by Kinimaka. It took another half hour before she slowed.

'Hey guys,' she said. 'Be careful. This looks like another trap.'

Drake craned his head to get a better look. Hayden's light was shining on another stone, this one depressed. Carefully, the whole team picked their way past without stepping on it and a look up revealed the edge of another portcullis. Drake shivered as he passed beneath.

Another fifteen minutes of walking brought them to a wide cavern. Hayden slowed and let out a long, deep breath. The team dispersed into the new space, spreading out carefully.

Ahead of them lay a field of sharp rock, a natural obstruction. They would have to pick their way through the pointed, spiky obstacles.

'Take your time,' Kerry said to all. 'See you on the other side.'

There was no simple path. Drake stepped over one ragged point, around another, and found himself faced by yet another row. He lifted a leg over the next, put his foot down in a few inches of space, and then paused. He wasn't even a quarter of the way through. Slowly, he picked his way forward. If he lost his balance here he was doomed, and it wasn't easy to keep. No steps were straightforward or uniform. He had to twist his body every time he moved forward and then pause in an unnatural position. Around the cavern the others were progressing too. Lee, to his left, fell over but got lucky, coming down where there were no spikes. He managed to pull himself up and dust himself off. Lee took a deep breath, meeting Kerry's eyes.

'Be careful,' she said. It was unnecessary, but it was a welcome comment.

They moved through the spike-filled arena. Drake passed the halfway mark and crouched to crab walk through a narrow gap. He could have crawled, but the rock would have punished his knees. He made it through. He looked at his team. Dahl and Kinimaka, the biggest, seemed to be having the most trouble threading their way through. They were lagging behind. Drake could have said something glib, something to piss the big Swede off, but now was not the time. Nobody wanted to leave this cavern with broken bones.

Kerry reached the other side first. There was an empty space of perhaps eight feet before the tunnel started again. Lee came next and then Danielle. The Ghost Squadron were taking their time, though Mai stepped as lithely as a gazelle. At the back, Dahl and

Kinimaka made out they were checking for a tail before resuming. Drake thought it wasn't actually a bad idea.

'Why don't you stay behind a bit?' he said. 'And we'll carry on. If anyone is following us, it'd be good to catch them in the middle of the spiky field.'

'Is that its official name?' Hayden asked with a smile.

'If only there were an official guidebook,' Drake said.

In moments, they were off again, slipping through the tunnel. It didn't change, but continued to wind ever on. This time Mai took the lead, but didn't come across any traps. After a while, the tunnel widened as if it was coming to another cavern. Drake picked his way carefully forward. The entire team was laced with tension.

Mai emerged into another wide cavern. This one was high, with a domed ceiling. It stood perhaps thirty feet long and, at its far end, Drake could make out a small object.

'It's the chest,' Kerry said with relief. 'We've found it.'

Lee was the first one to start forward. He moved with a grin on his face.

But Kerry suddenly grabbed his shoulders, dragging him back. *'Wait!'*

CHAPTER THIRTY FIVE

Drake blinked in confusion. He saw Kerry grab Lee, heard her words, but couldn't see anything wrong. Then Kerry gestured at the cavern's walls.

'Look,' she said. 'I see holes.'

Drake focused. He saw a series of holes all the way down the cavern about chest height. He knew immediately what they were for. The floor, he saw, comprised three different shaped tiles. Some patterns were repeated. He looked around, seeing the various rocks scattered around the floor. After a moment, he walked over and picked one up.

Drake walked back to just before the start of the tile pattern and threw the rock a few feet. It landed on a square tile.

Nothing happened.

Drake repeated the pattern, this time aiming for a round tile. The rock smashed down hard, rolling off. Again, nothing happened.

'Well, there's only one more chance,' Kenzie said. 'The triangle shape.'

Drake was already on it. He collected another rock, went back, and this time aimed for the triangular shaped tile. He missed it much to several groans. Tried again. This time, his aim was true. The rock hit the triangle shape full on.

There was a sudden displacement of air. Something flew from both sides of the cavern, a small dart. Both darts struck the far wall and fell off. If a person had been standing there, they would have done serious damage.

Kerry took a deep breath. 'One more trap before the chest,' she said. 'The makers will hope the uninitiated just run straight for the chest.'

Lee, who had been doing just that, gave her a sheepish smile. Kerry looked ahead. 'Right,' she said. 'Stay off the triangular tiles.'

Cautiously, the group traversed the cavern. They took it easy, wary even of stepping on the correct tiles. What if the pattern changed halfway across? Drake wouldn't put anything devious past the Cerberim. So they made their way with winces and cringes and a great deal of shuddering. Bravely, Mai took the lead, being the first to tread on the next row of tiles. She made it across to the far side without incident.

Drake was the last to step onto safe ground. By that time, Kerry was already approaching the chest. Drake got a good look at it before she fell to her knees. It was the same as all the others.

Danielle and James joined her. Together, the archaeologists opened the new chest.

And reached inside. The aides joined them expectantly. Kerry held up a scroll and Danielle shined a torch on it.

'We have a new clue,' she said. 'And it's a bit short. *With your penultimate scroll, start your search in Old Manila with the ancient Endac fountain.*'

'That's interesting,' James said.

'A couple of remarkable words in so short a sentence,' Kerry said. 'First,' and her words shook with excitement. 'It says *penultimate*. That means we're nearly there.' She looked up and around, eyes shining. The archaeologists and aides gave her a similar look back.

'Aren't you glad you stayed now?' she said.

Immediately, though, her face went serious, and she looked guilty. Her love for her job, her words, had got away from her and she'd forgotten about Jack. She looked away, back to the scroll.

'Also,' she said. 'The scroll says the words "start your search." It doesn't give a location for the chest. Which kind of suggests a bit of a treasure hunt.'

'What are we even looking for at this Endac fountain?' Danielle asked.

'I guess we'll see when we get there,' Kerry said. 'I'm guessing there will be a clue on the fountain itself.'

'Or a dead end,' James said ominously.

Kerry gave him an exasperated look. 'Why would you say that?'

'Sorry,' James muttered. 'It's how my brain works.'

Kerry set about making the scroll safe and picking up the now empty chest. She turned with it in her arms. 'Time for the return journey,' she said fretfully, and Drake knew it would be just as hard and risky getting back as it had been to get here.

He jumped on the comms. 'Dahl? Are we clear back there?'

'Safe and sound.'

He nodded at Kerry. 'No worries,' he said.

They started to pick their way back through the booby-trapped tiles. At one point, James misstepped and trod on a triangular tile, but pulled back fast enough so that the dart shot right by him. Luckily, it didn't hit anyone else. The archaeologist gave everyone a worried, embarrassed smile.

'I should know better,' he said.

They had all frozen on the spot. Now they restarted. They successfully negotiated the cavern of tiles and then found themselves back at the spiky field, which proved as difficult to negotiate back as it had been previously. They took their time. Eventually, they were across and traversing the long tunnels that housed the portcullis traps. Soon, they were beyond them and staring at the entrance.

'Blessed sunlight,' Hayden said.

Drake felt the same. Together, the team of adventurers headed for the light.

CHAPTER THIRTY SIX

Dahl's voice hissed over the comms.
'We have company, coming from the east.'
Drake cursed. 'Have they seen you?'
'Not yet?'
'Are they headed for the volcano?'
'Definitely.'
Mai, also ranging out far, joined in the conversation. 'I'm counting... well, there's more than I can count among the trees. At least ten, probably more.'
Drake looked over at the aides, the archaeologists. They shouldn't be in another fight. 'Are they armed?'
'All armed with guns.'
'Then it's a run,' Drake said. 'We have to run from them.'
Kerry looked over, having overheard that last part. 'You're kidding me?'
Drake spoke up. 'Listen to me, everyone. The enemy has arrived. They're armed. Our scouts have spotted them, so we're gonna have to run. Follow me.'
Drake got the enemy's position off Dahl and chose a route. The island, being flat and barren, offered little concealment, but the lava flows were deep in

parts and might come in useful. He started by leading them to the east of their boat, hoping to slip right past the enemy. Dahl kept him apprised of their position.

The entire team left the cave behind and slipped into the crevice of a lava flow. It ran for several hundred metres. They climbed out the other side and then descended into another, this one quite wide. Again they crossed it, climbed up out the other side and then had to navigate a patch of flat ground to the next flow. They ran as hard as they could, heads down.

Dahl's voice on the comms. 'They're nearing the cave area. Get your heads down.'

Drake made the next crevice in the landscape and jumped down. The others streamed in after him. 'Lie low,' he told them. 'No sound.'

They all sprawled out along the bottom of the crevice, not moving. Drake had his head to the ground, but watched carefully above. They weren't on the straight track to the cave, which he assumed the bad guys would take. With any luck, they'd pass right by them.

Soon enough, he heard voices. The enemy wasn't being subtle. Drake did not know their exact position. They could be close or far. He heard them clearly, though.

'See the cave?' One said. 'We've made it.'

'Maybe they're inside.'

'Be ready, men. I want these bastards to suffer for what they've done.'

'Oh, they will, boss. They will.'

Drake cast his glance over the group. James had

his eyes closed. Kerry and Danielle were breathing shallowly, looking at each other with wide eyes. His own team was flat out, but coiled and ready to pounce. If they were found, they still didn't want to be taken.

Dahl's voice came over the comms. 'They're approaching the caves. Where are you?'

'Do I need to start slowly taking them out?' Mai asked.

Drake didn't dare speak. The scouts would understand. He lay there, tensed up, listening.

'Are we going straight in?' An enemy asked.

'Do you see any signs that they've been here?' The leader's voice asked.

'Actually, I do,' One man said. 'There's an empty bottle of water right here.'

Drake shook his head. One of the aides being careless.

'So they're either inside or have already gone.' The leader let out a harsh curse. 'Damn it. Well, maybe we'll catch them on their way out.'

'And we kill them?'

'Remember what I said. I want the archaeologists alive. The rest... you can kill.'

Drake looked across at the archaeologists, all huddled together. Their eyes were wide, scared. Drake put a finger to his lips.

Minutes passed. The enemy was clearly advancing to the cave entrance. Drake had to rely on Dahl's intel, and wouldn't move until he got the all clear.

As if on cue, the Swede's voice came across the airwaves. 'They've slowed right next to the cave. Don't look up. They're searching the landscape.'

Drake knew this was the deadliest moment. He lay in tension and strain, unmoving, wishing he didn't have to hide. It wasn't in his nature. But lying low was the only option. Even if they didn't have civilians along, they'd have to hide since the enemy was fully armed. It occurred to him then that, for the future, they'd have to develop some network where they could easily acquire guns on a foreign job. But that wouldn't be as easy as it sounded.

The pressure built. They lay in utter silence. Jed, the aide, was shivering. James still had his eyes closed.

'They're searching,' Dahl said. 'Good luck.'

'I'm as close as I can get,' Mai said. 'If they find you, I can probably disarm the closest asshole and grab a gun.'

That was something. Drake waited, the seconds ticking by like slow molasses. He was ready for anything, ready to uncoil and strike. If Mai attacked, he would attack.

Tension surrounded them. Drake was surprised the bad guys couldn't see and feel it emanating from the crevice in waves.

Dahl kept them apprised. 'They aren't venturing far. They're still looking though, but unenthusiastically. The leader is waiting by the cave entrance. He seems to be a doer. He's nervous, wanting to get on with the job. It was his idea for his men to scan their surroundings, but I think he just wants to get inside that cave.'

'He's calling them back,' Mai said. 'They're readying to go inside.'

More minutes oozed by. Drake was uncomfortable

as hell, the rock unyielding. He saw Danielle stretch, shook his head at her. They couldn't afford any sound at all.

'This is it,' Mai said. 'They're all getting their flashlights out and heading inside the cave. I'm counting nineteen men. Even we might struggle against nineteen armed men. Yeah, they're all gone. Oh, wait.'

Drake licked his lips, badly wanting to move a muscle.

'Damn it, they've left a guard outside.'

Mai crouched in the shadow of a large rock. She hadn't moved in some time, blending with the landscape. This was what she did, what she had been trained to do from a young age. She waited, watching.

A young man with a big gun stood outside the cave entrance. He looked bored and pissed, and didn't really know where to look. In the end he stood facing away from her, watching the landscape and all the approaches.

Mai waited, counting the seconds. She wanted to make sure the bulk of the enemy had left the area and was firmly out of the picture. The young man searched from side to side, his eyes probably passing right over Drake's hiding place.

Mai stretched. Then she crept within the shadow of the large rock, moving forward. She was fifteen feet from the man. His gun was cradled in his right hand, the barrel pointed at the floor.

Mai advanced. She was light on her feet, making

no noise at all. The rocky ground helped. She was sure-footed, creeping from step to step. The movements were engrained in her, part of who she was.

The gap closed. Fifteen feet became ten, and then five.

Mai came up behind the man and looped an arm around his throat. She squeezed with crushing pressure. Immediately, he dropped his gun, then brought both hands up to fend her off. His fingertips dug into her skin. Mai didn't feel it. She exerted every ounce of her strength to squeeze his throat.

She wasn't aiming to make him unconscious here. These guys weren't playing, and she didn't want a survivor waking up behind them. She had to be swift, severe, and precise. She held her position for some time until the guy's struggles weakened. Finally, he sank to the ground.

Mai picked up his gun. 'Clear,' she said, perfectly calm.

Drake gave the signal. Immediately, they all climbed to their feet, some groaning and stretching aching limbs. Drake's own limbs ached too, but he ignored that. He made sure everyone was on their feet.

'Quickly now,' he said.

The entire team scrambled up the slope into the open. Then they ran. They ran for the next lava flows and then the ones beyond that; they ran for their lives. Dahl and Mai joined them and soon the beach was in sight and their precious boats. They all piled in.

And escaped the island.

CHAPTER THIRTY SEVEN

The main boat got out of the area quickly.

Dahl impressed their urgency upon the captain, and they were soon underway, heading away from the Solomons. A short while later, Kerry went in and asked him to plot a course for Manila.

'It's going to take a while,' the man said.

'Better put your foot down,' Drake said with a grin.

'I'll do that,' the captain had become used to their ways by now. He turned to his charts, and Drake left him alone.

It did take a while. Days. The team sat around their cabin and waited it out. There was time to get together, to switch off for a while, to decompress. All this time, Drake kept a watch on their progress, making sure nobody was following them or trying to sneak up on them. The entire Ghost Squadron took turns watching, two at a time.

The night passed easily. The teams ate and then shared a few bottles of wine, content. At first they studied the clue but, it being so short, didn't offer a lot of insight. Kerry read about Manila and found information on the Endac fountain. She also pinpointed its location so they would be ready the moment their feet touched solid ground.

Drake and the rest of his team sat on comfy chairs, taking it all in their stride. He watched the aides and the archaeologists. They seemed to have taken the latest scare in their stride.

'Not long to go now,' Dahl said from Drake's right-hand side.

Drake nodded. 'We're headed for the penultimate clue,' he said. 'We have to keep these people safe for just a little while longer.'

'It was close back there.'

'Those guys aren't as good as they think they are.'

'They'll know we bested them by now. Killed one of them. It won't go down well.'

'What more can they do? They were already planning to kill us and abduct the archaeologists.'

Dahl sat back. 'Good point.'

'Coming from you, that's a massive compliment.'

'Don't get used to it.'

'As if,' Drake sipped his wine and watched the room, still taking in people's emotions. Kenzie, Hayden and Kinimaka were chatting easily with the archaeologists who were seated in a little huddle, away from the others. Maybe they were discussing the mission. Drake turned to Dahl.

'How are you finding the new venture, my friend?'

'Spear Solutions? Too early to tell. But I like the idea. I like what we're doing. We just have to get the right jobs. Make our name. Then we can choose what we do and when we do it.'

'We already have a good name with the right people.'

'True. But this is a new endeavour. And not something we're familiar with. I mean, owning a business? I'm just glad we have a good secretary.'

'Yeah, Sabrina is top-notch. Have you heard from her lately?'

'A few emails. Jobs are popping up left, right and centre. I think, in the future, we may have to split our forces.'

Dahl nodded. 'In hindsight, sending everyone on one mission wasn't the best idea.'

Drake could only smile. 'You live and learn.'

'Speaking of that,' Alicia leaned in from his other side. 'How the hell do these assholes keep finding us?'

'Tracker?' Dahl suggested.

'There could be something in someone's luggage,' Drake admitted. 'But it's more likely one of our number is a mole.'

Alicia nodded gravely. 'I'm guessing it's Mai.'

Drake smiled and shook his head at her. 'You're not funny. My guess is it's Jed or Lee.'

'I'm with you there,' Alicia said. 'And I've been watching them since we came on board. Neither of them has sneaked off into the shadows.'

'The days are long,' Drake said. 'We can't watch them every minute. And if they're good, which they clearly are, they will find a way. They could even text the info across. I mean, look at Lee. He's texting now.'

'Maybe we should go take a look at his phone,' Alicia suggested.

'We're here to protect these people,' Drake said. 'Not badger them. We have to trust them.'

'I'll have a talk with Kerry,' Dahl said. 'Maybe she can do the badgering.'

They drifted from the subject, discussing something new. The night waxed around them for a while, and then Drake started to get tired. He'd checked with the captain earlier and had been told the journey would take another two days, barring bad weather. They'd been lucky so far on this trip, encountering only a couple of squalls.

Manila moved closer hour by hour. The boat never stopped cutting through the relatively calm waters apart from when the captain needed sleep, and he didn't seem to need a lot of that.

Drake waited for the day when the sun would dawn over Manila.

CHAPTER THIRTY EIGHT

The boat docked in Manila under a hot midday sun. The archaeologists, the aides, and the Ghost Squadron were waiting for the exact moment it docked so they could resume their mission.

Drake disembarked first. He strode ahead through the crowds, searching for their aggressors. The entire team was on alert, flanking the archaeologists and the aides as they made their way along the long dock. Manila was located on the eastern shore of Manila Bay and is a highly urbanised city. It is part of an ancient trade route, and had been an important point on the map for centuries. For now, Drake just saw the hustle and bustle of a hectic, active city and knew it would be hard to keep track of their civilians and watch out for the bad guys.

But they were seven strong. They would have to be enough. And Mai still carried her new gun, now concealed, which ought to give them a little more advantage.

As a pack, they pressed through the crowd. Kerry had entered the address for the Endac fountain into Google Maps and was now following the route closely. It appeared to be a twenty-minute walk through busy streets.

And all that time, they would be exposed.

Drake wondered if the enemy actually had proper descriptions of them. He didn't think so. They didn't seem entirely organised or hands-on and might not even have the resources to get proper IDs for their own enemies. Drake thought they were winging it.

Kerry led the civilians through Manila, closing in on the fountain.

The sun beat down hard and there was a nice cool breeze wafting in from the sea. Drake walked through an ocean of smells, from car and boat exhaust to fresh paint and fried meat and fish. Stalls were everywhere, and gaudy shops with their doors thrown open.

People shouted their wares or called to each other. Car horns beeped. Somewhere a dog barked incessantly. Drake watched as many people as he could, but saw nothing untoward. Soon, Kerry announced they were just a few minutes away from the fountain.

Drake looked harder, knowing if the enemy were here, they would be close to the fountain itself.

They turned left down a side street and then right along a much broader street. Soon, the road widened, and they were entering a large square surrounded by three storey high blocky buildings. The square was chaotic, a mass of meandering people, but there was no mistaking the fountain at its centre.

The Endac fountain was a large, round representation of two horses pulling a chariot with a helmeted man inside. The man held a spear and was shouting. In the other hand he held the reins. The horses were leaping forward, the entire depiction giving the impression of a dynamic, vibrant scene.

Drake watched the perimeters as Kerry and the other civilians walked towards it. They cut their way through the crowds as if they deserved to be there, then took different points of the fountain and started to search. Earlier, Drake had taken the liberty of giving Kerry some comms, knowing they'd be working amongst a sizeable crowd.

'Kerry,' he said surreptitiously. 'Let me know if you find anything.'

'*When*,' she said. 'Let's be positive about this.'

He agreed, but didn't answer. His team spread out throughout the square, watching for anything suspicious. Steadily, Kerry and her crew started their work.

Drake walked a set route, crossing the square slowly from left to right. It was a constant stream of unfamiliar faces, people coming and going about their business. There were two police officers to one side, also looking around, but they soon disappeared. Drake saw a road nearby and monitored the stream of cars, but no one slowed.

Kerry and the others worked their magic. Drake saw them bending and examining the fountain. They searched the top and the sides and then bent in to study the statue itself, looking closely at the stunning architecture.

The square had three entrances. Dahl, Mai, and Alicia were stationed at them, guarding them. They saw everyone who entered, everyone who left. Some time passed. Drake counted the minutes. They were exposed out here, and of course, looking a little suspicious.

Kerry's voice cut through the noise. 'I'm staring right now at a Cerberim symbol. One of the snarling demon faces.'

Drake couldn't help but grin. He may look odd to passers-by, but it felt good to him. He started walking towards her. 'Let's see.'

It had been cut into the western wall of the fountain and stood amongst other more agreeable carvings. Drake saw the usual demonic face, but that was not all he saw. 'There's an arrow,' he said.

Kerry nodded. 'I noticed that, too. See where it points?'

Bending, Drake followed the direction of the arrow with his eyes. It pointed directly at what appeared to be an ancient staircase set on a close-by building.

'Up there?' he asked.

'That's what I'm thinking.'

Drake straightened. He checked the direction again. The arrow was indeed pointing at the staircase, and Kerry seemed convinced. The other archaeologists took their turns.

Kerry was already walking towards the staircase. Drake slowed her down. 'Let's all go at the same time,' he said.

She looked impatient, but stopped and waited. The aides were also crowded around the fountain. Drake checked his team and saw they were all in position. Soon, both Danielle and James were straightening.

'To the staircase,' Danielle said.

It was a short walk across the square to the staircase. It was old and made of stone and led up the side of a building before turning left at the top, where it ended in a walkway. They would be exposed as they walked up. Nobody else was using it, but there were no signs to say it was off limits. Kerry wasn't bothered either way. She stepped on to the staircase, scanning the wall beside it for more clues.

Drake followed her up, his eyes also drawn to the wall. He berated himself. His eyes ought to be turned outward, watching the crowd, but he was fascinated. The wall was smooth, though, at least where he was looking. Both Danielle and James came after him, also intent on their task. Drake saw Mai come to stand near the foot of the staircase.

Kerry crept upwards, a slow riser at a time. She checked the risers themselves, too. The din of passing people still filled the air, and the smells drifted up here in a heady mix. Two minutes later, Kerry ran her hand across the wall.

'It's nothing,' she said after a while.

They were halfway up, Kerry progressing slowly but steadily. By now, the aides were also on the stairway and conducting their own search. Drake guessed the more pairs of eyes, the better. He added his own, hoping to spot something Kerry missed.

She was three quarters of a way up and still going. Drake was sweating from more than the blasting sun. More time passed. They weren't attracting any undue attention, and the comms were quiet, which was a good thing.

Finally, Kerry came to the top. Almost immediately, she stiffened. 'What's this?' she said to herself.

Drake overheard and looked over her shoulder.

And there it was. One more demonic face staring back at him, set into the wall at the top of the staircase. Kerry bent to examine it. Drake saw another arrow, this one pointing to the left.

Kerry followed its direction.

'It seems to point down there,' she said. 'Do you see that old doorway?'

Drake copied her. He, too, stared back down into the square and saw the doorway in question. It was narrow and arched and seemed to bear several carvings up and down its frame.

'I see it.'

Kerry let Danielle and James examine the new carving. Everyone concurred the arrow was pointing at the doorway. Next, Kerry started down the stairway much faster than she'd ascended, almost pushing the aides out of her way in her haste.

She reached the square and headed for the doorway. Crowds surrounded her almost immediately. Drake lost her for a moment and had to jump on the comms.

'Kerry, slow down. I can't see you.'

From the staircase, he now saw the top of her head. She was looking back at him, waving, standing out from the crowd. Drake shook his head. He guessed you couldn't teach a civilian to blend in. He hurried over to her.

'Stay close,' he said. 'They want to abduct you.'

'Sorry.'

Soon, everyone had crowded around the old doorway. It wasn't difficult to pick out the next symbol.

A scowling, demon-like face graced the very top of

the frame, in the centre of the doorway. It had horns, and it had sharply slanted eyes. This time, there was no arrow.

Kerry looked at the door.

'I guess we go inside.'

CHAPTER THIRTY NINE

Once through the door, they found a small, drafty room and a ragged hole in the ground. The hole led to a set of old, broken steps that ran deep into the recesses of the room. Kerry didn't hesitate. She took out her flashlight, set herself, and then started down. Drake followed closely, shining his own torch around. Kerry took it at a slow pace, wary of traps, but didn't let up. She was fully invested in this quest.

The stairs went on for a while, eventually ending in a series of narrow passages. The passages were so small Drake could barely walk through without turning sideways. It was dirty and rough and dank. The team spread out in single file, wary, cautious. Kerry moved ahead steadily.

The minutes passed slowly. The passage wound on and on. Drake shivered. It was cold down here and the sweat on his face had turned into cool droplets. He wiped it away. After a while, the passage widened slightly and, ahead, carved into the wall, he saw several sets of niches.

And in the niches, robe-wrapped bodies.

'My god, we're in a crypt,' Kerry breathed.

Drake looked left and right. The niches went on into the distance and were five or six rows high on both walls. There had to be dozens of bodies here. At some point in the far reaches of time, this had been an important place.

'Keep going,' he said.

They pushed through the crypt, ignoring the shrouded bodies to both sides. Dust hung in the air, and Drake couldn't quite push from his mind what that dust might contain. He kept going, breathing shallowly.

The entire team progressed through the crypt, which stretched for some distance. Nobody spoke. Beyond the crypt, they came to a fast-flowing river. Everyone stopped on the rocky banks.

'How the hell are we supposed to get across that?' Alicia said.

Drake was wondering the same. It was powerful and made a surging, rushing noise. 'I guess they don't need traps when they've got this,' he said.

But Kerry had already spotted something. She pointed, drawing Drake's eyes. Across the far side, waiting in a niche, stood another chest. Kerry made an impatient noise.

Drake eyed the water. 'Shit,' he said.

They brought out rope and decided quickly who should venture across. They decided that person should be big and sturdy, so really it came down to a choice between Dahl and Kinimaka. Neither looked too pleased at being nominated. In the end it was Kinimaka who volunteered, stripping off his jacket and boots and everything except his boxer shorts. He stood on the banks of the river, looking forlorn as Alicia and Kenzie tied the rope around him and then took good hold.

He turned towards the river. Alicia gave him a swat. 'Good luck.'

'Thanks.'

Kinimaka waded out, shivering as the water struck him. He wasted no time, striding through the rushing water as fast as he could. The rush was only about five feet wide, but the swell of surging water slowed him down as it tried to destroy his balance. Alicia and Kenzie held on tightly to the rope, anchoring him. Kinimaka pushed on.

And slipped. Water rushed over his head as Kinimaka floundered. Alicia tugged the rope hard, sliding towards the river. For a moment, Drake lost all sight of the big Hawaiian as the man tumbled to one side. He ran to help with the rope, but Alicia and Kenzie had it covered. They hauled on it, dragging Kinimaka to his feet.

He rose to his knees, dripping water, and then to his feet. He was halfway across. Kinimaka took another step, staggering again. He almost stumbled, but caught himself, took another step. He was almost there. Alicia and Kenzie were pulling hard, keeping him upright against the tumult. Kinimaka lunged the last few feet, dragged himself out of the flow and fell onto the other bank. He looked exhausted and totally soaked. Slowly, he dragged himself to his knees.

Kinimaka shook himself like a wet dog. He looked back at them across the river. 'I don't recommend it,' he said drily.

He squeezed the water out of his hair and boxers before moving again. Then he approached the chest. He fell to his knees before it and reached out. Drake could see the worry on Kerry's face and she couldn't help but call out, 'Be careful.'

Kinimaka dragged the chest clear of the niche and then opened the lid. He stared for a moment. 'Just the scroll,' he shouted out. 'Nothing different here.'

He reached inside and drew the scroll out and read it before turning to the group. 'I'm gonna read this out now,' he yelled above the roar of the water. 'In case I have a little mishap bringing it back.'

He moved to the edge of the water, reading the scroll. 'All right. It says *the final chest lies amid the old ruins and jungles near Quy Nhon in the old temple beneath. You must dig to reach the chest.*'

Kerry read it back to him. Danielle and James were taking notes, as ever. Kerry looked pleased that they had more work to do.

Kinimaka hefted the chest with the scroll inside it.

It was time to head back.

CHAPTER FORTY

They made it quickly through the passage and back up to daylight. By the time they returned to the square, it was mid-afternoon, and it was as busy as ever. The very first thing Mai saw was their enemy.

'It's the leader,' she said over the comms. 'I saw his face back on the island.'

The leader, surrounded by his men, was cutting his way through the square in the direction of the fountain. Luckily, for now, all their attention was focused on it. Soon, the leader was bending down to examine the stonework and ordering his men to do the same. Drake and the others tried to melt away in the crowd.

It was busy enough to do so. They blended with the people, didn't group together, and exited via a far street. The enemy was still examining the fountain as they left.

Drake headed back for the boat. It was clear, and had been for some time, that they had a rat in their midst. Someone was feeding the bad guys the clues. Today, they had been lucky. There could just as easily have been a big fight in the square.

Alicia was at his side. 'We have to do something about this.'

Drake shrugged. 'Mano already read out the next clue. He had to. Give me a moment.' He looked at Kerry and beckoned her over.

'We're convinced one of your team is feeding the clues to the enemy,' he told her. 'Who don't you trust?'

Her eyes were wide. 'I haven't worked with any of them before. It's my first time in southeast Asia. I like them all, respect them all, but... trust? No.'

'That really narrows it down,' Alicia said pointedly.

'How about we mitigate the damage?' Drake said. 'Could you discuss the clue just between you archaeologists?'

Kerry looked over at Jed and Lee, the remaining aides. 'You think it's one of them?'

'Honestly, I don't know. I'm just trying to lessen the impact here.'

'I can make that work.'

'Good, because we don't have a clue what the last clue means,' Alicia said. 'Which is acceptable. For now.'

'We'll get to work on it once we're on the boat,' Kerry said.

They returned to the boat, boarded, and set sail out of the harbour. Kerry announced that she, Danielle, and James were going to work on the clue alone, since it was so difficult and they needed all their concentration. Drake backed them up. Lee and Jed looked surprised, but not shifty, not miserable, and moved away as the archaeologists got into a huddle. Drake made sure his presence was known to the aides.

Maybe, this time, they'd get to the clue without the enemy on their tails.

The boat anchored once it was in deeper water, away from the city. The captain waited for them to work, smoking in his small cabin. Drake and the rest of the Ghost Squadron watched their environs and took the time to decompress. Kinimaka sat under a thick blanket, still shivering despite the heat of the day.

The archaeologists stayed in their huddle for the rest of the afternoon, but about the time Dahl, Kenzie and Hayden were breaking out the usual food and drink, Kerry came up for air. She caught Drake's eye and beckoned him over.

She whispered in his ear. 'We think we've cracked it. Quy Nhon is a lovely place in Vietnam. It's picturesque and old and renowned for an old ruined architectural site. We believe that's where the temple will be.'

'You worked all that out in just a few hours?'

'Once you pin down the site, it's not so difficult. There can only be one site. And, of course, once there we know what we're looking for.'

Drake nodded. 'Have you pinpointed the temple?'

'No, but the ruins will be obvious. The problem will be digging through the debris, looking for the Cerberim symbol.'

Drake looked over at Lee and Jed. Lee was watching him from the corner of his eye. Drake didn't trust him.

'Tell the captain not to mention our course to anyone,' he said. 'Keep it quiet.'

Kerry nodded and went off to the captain's cabin.

Before long, the boat was underway again, sailing further away from Manila. Drake and the others settled in for a long night and a longer journey before they docked in Vietnam. The waters were smooth, and the sun was just starting to set, casting a spreading crimson glow over the horizon. They had got lucky today, avoided battle and bloodshed. Drake considered it a welcome change. It was nice to get away from somewhere unscathed.

And they had gained something in the overall battle today.

They had compartmentalised the location of the next clue. Maybe, just maybe, that would give them the edge they needed. Every time they met the enemy, they were going in at a disadvantage – Mai being the only one of them with a gun. The enemy was always armed. Drake and the others had to overcome that obstacle on future missions.

For now, though, they were headed to Vietnam, and they had nothing to worry about. He turned to study the sunset.

CHAPTER FORTY ONE

Javier was fuming. He and his men had found the fountain. They'd located the demonic face and had followed the clues. The trouble was none of them were archaeologists and they just didn't know where they were going. They saw the faces; they saw the arrows, but didn't know how to interpret the clues. In the end, they all met back at the square, sweaty and annoyed. Javier did not know what to do next. He stationed his men around the place for a while, just in case the archaeologists and their retinue appeared. Nothing happened. The afternoon waned. Javier could barely contain his frustration. It appeared the archaeologists had beaten him again.

In and out before he got there.

Javier took his men back to the hotel and locked himself in his room. Once there, he swigged from the bottle of rum he'd brought and fished out his phone. It was a matter of seconds to jab in a speed dial number.

The call wasn't answered. Javier hadn't expected it to be, but he did expect a call back at the person's earliest convenience.

It happened twenty minutes later, just as Javier was downing his fourth rum. The phone buzzed, and he answered.

'You weren't there today,' Lee said.

Javier bit back a sharp curse. 'We were there,' he said with gravel in his voice. 'Just not on time.'

'We have a problem.'

Javier's hands turned into fists. 'What now?'

'They suspect someone of passing information on.'

'I'm surprised it took them this long to make that decision.'

'The protectors have been keeping themselves pretty aloof, out of the everyday decision making. Now, they've changed their minds, probably because of the risk.'

'So what are you saying, Lee?'

'Today, they didn't let the aides help in figuring out the clue. I have no idea where we're going.'

'But you do have the clue?'

Lee reeled it off. Javier copied it down. 'The last clue,' Javier mused. 'And we don't know what it means.'

'I'm sorry.'

And now Javier smiled. 'Don't worry about it, Lee. You've done well until now. I have another source.'

Lee was stunned into silence. Eventually, he said, 'Wh...what?'

'In my game, it pays to have contingencies. Now keep doing what you're doing. I may have need of you yet. And if you see us coming, attacking, help us.'

Lee agreed and ended the call. Javier now flicked through the contacts on his phone. When he found the right one, he grinned again.

'Perfect,' he said.

He made the call. The phone was answered on the

fifth ring. 'I don't have long,' the female voice said.

'This is our first contact,' Javier said. 'Lee has done well so far.'

'I saw what happened today and have been expecting your call.'

'Do you know the destination?'

'Yes, I helped work it out. Quy Nhon is a city in Vietnam. There are some ruins nearby. The temple will be there.'

Javier noted it all down. He was pleased and content with his own foresight. He had predicted all of this, and was still one step ahead.

'This is the last clue,' he said. 'We will come with all force. Be careful you don't get in the way. Oh, and Danielle?'

'Yes?'

'From this moment, pass on any information you think I might need.'

He ended the call before she could speak and then settled back, feeling much better. He thought about the next steps. They would need guns and ammo. They would need two helicopters and all the men they had. This would be the final confrontation.

Javier was going to win.

But then a new thought hit him like a hammer blow.

I have two helicopters. They have a boat.

If he could use the choppers to get to the ruins first. If he beat them to it…

That would work. And then he could find the final Underworld all by himself. It would deprive him of any vengeance, but it meant he would be victorious.

CHAPTER FORTY TWO

The boat was nearing Vietnam and the city, Quy Nhon. Drake and the others were packed and ready to disembark, ready for the drive through the city and the trek to the ruins, which apparently were a good half day's walk to the west. The boat docked easily and then they were off, looking for Ubers at the end of the dock. They would use the vehicles to get as close to the ruins as possible, but then there was a problem.

The ruins were ancient and, because of their remoteness to any town, unpopular. There wasn't a direct route, nothing on the internet, so the team was going to have to employ its own methods to properly pin them down. To that end, they had brought a drone along with them, a drone equipped with Lidar technology, so they could fly over the ruins and map a route through the forest to get there. Drake couldn't fault Kerry's pre-planning.

It was as they searched for their Ubers that Danielle called for a halt. She stood in front of them and then led them towards a quiet square. Kerry was staring at her in frustration. Drake couldn't understand the hold up.

Danielle rounded on them. 'It took us two days to sail here, right?'

Kerry nodded. 'So what?'

'That put us a whole day behind Javier.'

'Who the hell is Javier?' Alicia asked.

'The leader of our enemies. His name is Javier.'

Now Drake grew wary. He sent Hayden and Kinimaka out to watch their flanks. 'How would you know that?' Dahl asked.

'*You're* the traitor?' Kerry burst out. 'I never would have guessed it.'

'Not just me,' Kerry said, and nodded at Lee. 'Him too.'

Drake blinked in surprise. *Two* traitors? He hadn't expected it.

'But why?' Kerry couldn't get her head around it. 'People have died.'

'They have a hold over me. Something I'd prefer to stay a secret. Lee just did it for the money.'

By now, Lee was shrinking further and further back, eyes wide as if he was thinking about bolting. Kenzie stalled him by grabbing him by the back of the neck. Her expression told him to stay entirely still.

'They have a hold?' Kerry said. 'But you could have come to me. You didn't have to betray me.'

'I know, and it rankles with me. It hurts. It festers. That's why I'm telling you this, why I'm now turning against Javier. And if I don't do it, you'll never get close to the Underworld.'

'What do you mean?'

'Javier beat us by a full day. He now has an expert with him, someone who knew what they were doing and knew the ruins well. They found the temple, the passage underneath, and they found the chest.'

Kerry looked ready to cry. 'This isn't happening.'

'I'm sorry. I had no choice. Javier only brought me into all this a few days ago. Before that, it was all on Lee. I was the backup. But then you excluded Lee from the research process for Vietnam, so Javier called me.'

'And you were only too happy to oblige,' Kerry spat. 'To hand it all over.'

'I'm sorry. As I said, Javier has a hold on me. I didn't want to do it. And now I'm trying to prove that I *am* loyal.'

Drake narrowed his eyes at her. 'What do you mean?'

'By telling you all this. By telling you Javier made it to the ruins yesterday and found the scroll. And by revealing to you the new clue that leads finally to the Underworld. Maybe we can beat him there.'

Kerry looked like she was trying to be two people at once. Strong and understanding, but wild and annoyed. She was expectant, hopeful, frustrated.

'Javier told you the clue?'

'He was bragging to me this morning. And probably to Lee too. He had to get a few things together before going and needed my advice about the last clue. That's why he told it to me.'

'And we're supposed to just trust you now?' Mai asked.

'I never wanted to betray you. This is me making up for it. Please believe me.'

'All right,' Kerry breathed. 'Give us the last clue.'

'*Inside the Ivory Glacier in the land called New Zealand, you will find the great Ice Cave and the Underworld. Go carefully, for if you misstep, you will find only death.*'

Drake ran it through his head. It certainly sounded in the same vein as the other clues, which meant the Cerberim could have penned it. 'New Zealand?' he echoed.

Kerry was staring at Danielle as if she had two heads. 'How can we believe you?' She asked.

Danielle swept her arms to the west. 'You don't have to. Carry on. Go to the ruins. But by losing that time Javier will beat you to the Underworld. And you won't find the clue.'

Drake bit his top lip. It was an impossible choice. Here was a self-proclaimed traitor giving them special information about a new clue, the last clue, about the whereabouts of the Underworld. Everything they had gone through had come down to this.

Kerry turned to him. 'What do you think?'

He studied Danielle, the rawness in her face, the despair in her eyes. 'I believe her,' he said. 'I think she's trying to do the right thing.'

'You have to hurry,' Danielle said.

Drake turned to Lee. 'What do you have to say for yourself?'

The young man didn't know where to look. He just shrugged. 'She's right,' he said. 'Javier didn't give me the new clue, but he has it.'

Kerry cursed.

Drake listened to the input from his team. It matched his own thoughts. They all believed Danielle was telling the truth. 'She didn't even have to say anything,' Mai said. 'We could have blithely explored the ruins to find them empty.'

'That's true,' Kerry said. 'And she'd have kept her

secret.' She turned around. 'Right, everyone, let's head back to the boat.'

'What are we gonna do about this one?' Kenzie gave Lee a shake.

'Kill him,' Alicia said. She didn't mean it, but Lee didn't know that.

Drake looked like he was considering it. Lee stared at him, legs so rubbery he could barely stand. 'We'll take him with us,' he said at last. 'Lee, are you going to give us any trouble?'

Lee shook his head wildly. 'I won't make a sound.'

'If you annoy us, you're going overboard,' Dahl told him. 'Nostrils first.'

Lee nodded. Drake turned away and motioned for Kerry to lead the way.

'To New Zealand,' he said.

'To New Zealand,' she repeated.

CHAPTER FORTY THREE

'First, we need to find an ivory coloured glacier,' Kerry said.

They were seated around the table as their boat motored towards New Zealand. Kerry opened her laptop and started looking at images. It wasn't hard to get a list of the New Zealand glaciers and, comparatively, there weren't even that many of them.

Drake and the others watched Kerry and James work. They hadn't invited Danielle to help, and the archaeologist now sat glumly in one corner. Lee was close to her. The traitorous pair looked sorry for themselves and beaten.

The voyage to New Zealand continued. Kerry announced they would need specialist equipment to climb the glaciers once they arrived. They'd have to dock somewhere with a good supply of shops. The captain said that wouldn't be a problem.

The hours passed. The teams prepared. Kerry found the ivory coloured glacier and started using satellite images to find a cave entrance. By the time they'd reached New Zealand, she had a glacier, a cave and had mapped out a route from the town the captain told her they were going to dock in.

Drake was impressed. Kerry and James had wasted no time, and were fully prepared. Hayden had been part of the group too, offering her experience, but, in her own words, had felt pretty superfluous.

The boat docked, and they disembarked. They found the right shops to make their purchases and transport to take them to the foot of the glacier. They bought ice grips, ice axes, crampons, and ropes, as they knew they'd be roped together up there. They bought ladders to cross crevasses and specialist boots for the ice grips. Drake had done some glacier training when he was with the army and explained how they'd have to use crampons on their boots to dig into the ice underfoot. It would be a hard slog, but the glacier wasn't classified as a particularly dangerous one.

They started out from a snow-swept, ice-filled parking area and started making their way across a frozen tundra. Nobody expected an easy trek. It was going to test all their strength just to get to the glacier. They did not know where Javier and his men were, had no idea of their progress. And they sure as hell didn't want to bump into them on the glacier.

But none of that deterred them.

They were here, approaching the underworld of the Cerberim. This was the site of the great treasure. Nothing could have held them back.

Drake, being the only one with experience, led the way. He knew to look out for crevasses, pitfalls, and told them how to kick into the snow with each step and feel the teeth of the crampons bite into the ice. They were roped together for safety as they traversed the ice-laden glacier.

The air was bitingly cold. There was a soft breeze too that wasn't welcome. It blew flurries of snow into Drake's eyes so that his eyelashes were coated. After they'd been climbing for half an hour, he turned to Kerry.

'How close are we?'

The others huddled around, trying to stay warm.

'Shouldn't take more than another half hour to get to the cave,' she said. 'It's not too far.'

Drake led them on. Underfoot, so long as they used the ice grips, it wasn't too treacherous. Ahead, he saw a narrow crevasse coming up and bypassed it without need of the ladders. In fact, he hoped never to have to use them. The ladders would only slow them down. Drake stopped as a couple of intense gusts of wind scoured the landscape, putting his head down.

'This is fun,' Alicia cried out.

Drake shared her sentiments, but said nothing. They were approaching a steep stretch, and he needed all his concentration. He made sure his boots were firmly embedded in the ice before moving on, felt someone behind him slip. When he turned, James was picking himself up and dusting off. Other than embarrassment, he was fine. Drake took a moment to check on Kinimaka. Mano was the clumsy one, but seemed fine so far today.

The journey continued. Drake felt hungry and thirsty, but didn't want to stop on the exposed ice. When he came to the lee of a small hill, he bundled them into it and paused briefly.

'We're gonna need our energy,' he said. 'Eat and drink as fast as you can.'

They fuelled up. Kerry reckoned they were about fifteen minutes from their destination. The sky was blue and clear, the surrounding landscape glaringly white. They started off again, this time with their expectations high. Drake at the front and Dahl at the back kept their eyes open for unwanted company, but saw no one.

It was twenty minutes later when the ice cave came into view. On seeing it, Drake dropped low, just in case, but there was no sign of sentries. No sign that Javier had beaten them here, either. They approached the cave entrance cautiously.

'Let's get these ropes off,' Drake said.

Soon, they were ready to go inside. Mai, holding the only gun, went first. Drake and Kerry followed her. Dahl brought up the rear with Kenzie. They ducked into the cave and started walking.

It was a stupendous journey. The ice tunnel refracted all around them and the colours were insane. Drake saw turquoises, deep greens, light blues and reds. The bending tunnel shone with all manner of colours.

It was slippery underfoot. They couldn't wear the crampons on their way to a potential fight. They stepped slowly, ducking when the tunnel ceiling came down, sliding through when it narrowed. For the most part, though, the tunnel took them one way with relative ease.

Drake lost track of the amount of time they crept through the ice tunnel. Mai, ahead, was aware of possible sentries, and took her time, but came across no one.

They came to a bend in the tunnel. Drake saw a

different quality to the lights on the walls. At the same time, he heard the indistinct murmur of voices. Ahead, Mai stopped instantly.

The light on the walls was the reflection of flashlights. Drake cursed silently. Someone – no doubt Javier – was already here.

He moved up to Mai's shoulder. Together, they took a careful look around the corner.

And felt their jaws drop to the floor.

CHAPTER FORTY FOUR

It stopped them in their tracks.

Drake saw an immense cavern stretching up into darkness further than the eye could see. The walls glistened under the intense glare of many flashlights. The entire cavern was a mass of wealth and riches.

It took the breath away. Drake saw a mountain of gold, glittering and shimmering. He saw piles of rubies and emeralds, no doubt plundered from their owners. There were glistening diamonds, some the size of a fist. He saw an array of swords and shields, some battered and even blood red, arranged on the floor. Other gemstones reflected their incredible radiance. Purples and yellows and orange colours. Some he didn't even recognise. There were heaps of shimmering goblets, masses of jewellery, every facet catching the light. Drake's eyes were filled with wonder. He saw unopened chests resplendent with treasure, open chests with their sparkling content spilling out. Wherever a flashlight illuminated the cavern, riches shone with iridescent majesty.

This was the Underworld of the Cerberim. Their treasure horde.

Drake tried to get past the wonder. The enemy was already among the treasures. They were standing around and rooting through and just gazing in plain wonder. It was possible they hadn't been here that long. It made sense. Drake tapped Mai's shoulder and pulled back. He left her on guard and then faced the rest of the team.

'Lots of treasure,' he said. 'Lots of bad guys. Yeah, they're already here. And we're in their way. I suggest we come up with a plan of action quickly.'

Alicia looked and then returned. 'They're incredibly distracted,' she said. 'They haven't even posted any guards. And they're spread out. I think we can creep in there and cancel them. It's dark. Even if they see us among them, they'll think we're part of the same team.'

Drake liked the idea. If they moved quickly, if they dispersed fast among the enemy, they wouldn't notice the extra shadows.

'Everyone pick a man,' he said. 'Although we're probably gonna have to take down two each.'

The Ghost Squadron slipped into the treasure cave quietly and carefully, sticking to the deeper shadows. They then crept until they were among the treasure, standing close to an enemy. The sudden influx of new figures didn't register to Javier's men. They were busy gazing at the treasure, at each other, at Javier for direction. They appeared to be struck with wonder. Drake knew some of the reason they hadn't posted a sentry and were now standing around awestruck was complacency. They weren't a professional unit.

He left the civilians behind and gave his team time to reach their positions. There would have to be a signal. He saw Javier rooting through a mass of emeralds and then picking up streams of jewellery. Javier was grinning from ear to ear, thinking he'd won the day. His men were watching him and, seeing as the pressure was off, standing easily.

Drake saw his team move into position, standing close to their targets. They had turned off their flashlights and were all watching him, relying on the torches of the enemy for light. Drake raised an arm.

And then brought it down in a sudden strike.

The Ghost Squadron attacked. They needed to take out two enemies each. Drake battered a man around the head, watched him slip to the floor, before turning instantly to the man standing beside him. This guy he disabled with two quick throat strikes and then a jab to the eyes. The guy folded, incapable of action. Around the room, his team did the same, taking out the enemy with just a couple of blows.

But not everything ran perfectly. Some blows didn't work, some missed their targets. Javier's men fought back, hard.

Drake moved on to a third opponent after kicking his second in the throat. This man had a handgun and was pointing it at Drake's head. Javier had a couple of extra men. Drake threw himself behind a pile of gemstones before the man fired.

A gunshot filled the air. The gemstones jumped up where the bullet hit, one of them shattering. Drake felt the bullet pass him by, flying close to his head. He rolled. The pile of stone was big enough to give him enough space to evade the next bullet, and then he was up, hurling stones at the attacker.

The man ducked. Drake used the distraction to

jump at him, kicked him in the gun arm, and watched the weapon fly away. He noted its position. He took out the guy with three swift blows. Then, he ran to pick up the gun.

Javier was suddenly before him, weapon levelled at his chest.

Around the room, Dahl picked up his opponent and hurled him straight at a second man. The clash was huge and bone breaking; the shrieks piercing. Two guns fell from the collision and ended up in Dahl's hands. He quickly shot a third opponent. Kinimaka brought his huge hands smashing down on to one man's head, then whirled and crashed into another. Neither man could resist. They both went down hard. Alicia and Kenzie crushed their opponents with killer attacks, taking them out in seconds. Mai was a devastating whirlwind, moving among her enemies with deadly skills. Hayden thought quickly and stole her opponent's gun before he knew what was happening. He was twice as shocked when she turned and shot him with it.

Drake faced Javier amid the madness.

'Give it up,' the Yorkshireman said. 'It isn't worth your life.'

'It's you who's about to die. You and all your team.'

'Read the room, pal. You've already lost.'

Javier blinked, glancing between shadows. The flashlights were bucking and spinning and roving across the entire cavern. It seemed like the lights had gone wild, intermittently picking out piles of treasure and weapons and then the sides of the gleaming cavern.

'I deserve this,' he said. 'I already own it.'

'Not in my book, you don't.'

'Tell your people to stand down. Tell them, or I'll shoot you in the head.'

Drake gauged the situation. He wasn't close enough to disarm the man. He'd definitely get a shot off first. Drake inched closer. Maybe he could get close enough to strike.

'Stay where you are.'

'I'm not calling off the attack,' Drake said.

'Then you'll die,' Javier raised his weapon.

Something came flickering through the iridescent light. It was long and sharp and curved. Drake saw it quivering as it flew, lights sparkling off its blade, and then it sliced firmly into Javier's head. To the left, Alicia was standing on top of the pile of weapons, looking like a conqueror, and she had thrown a sword at Javier.

The sword penetrated Javier's skull and sent him instantly to the floor. The blade quivered in his head. The gun fell nervelessly to the ground. Drake winced. It wasn't a good way to go. Around the cave, Javier's men were too embattled to notice that their leader was gone.

Dahl and Kinimaka punished their opponents hard, sending more men into oblivion. They had taken up guns by now too and, where the lights showed irrefutably that they faced an enemy, they were using them. One by one, the enemy died.

Hayden traded shots with two men. They had ducked behind a row of steel chests, and were occasionally raising their heads like meerkats and firing off a wild shot. Alicia grappled with a big man on top of the pile of weapons, slipping and sliding precariously. Kinimaka and Dahl had also ducked out of sight as more gunshots crisscrossed the cavern. The flashlights wavered invariably, picking out random scenarios.

Drake used the darkness to close in on an opponent. He crept through it, hugging it, keeping his head down. The man in question was hiding behind a pile of emeralds, peeking out occasionally, but doing very little else. Drake crawled around the pile and targeted him, opening fire. When he did so, another enemy rose out of the darkness.

The guy had an Uzi. Drake's eyes flew wide. He had no chance. It was the darkness, the total blanketing, flickering darkness. It made you feel deranged. He faced the gun and watched the man's finger tighten on the trigger.

Mai flew in like a demon, whipping in from the left and whirling to the right. Her hands were like fast knives, striking and slicing. Incredibly, the guy was dead on his feet before he even realised it. Still standing there thinking he was alive, eyes lifeless, finger still on the trigger but unable to do anything.

The man folded in on himself, slithering to the ground.

Mai faced Drake. 'You okay?'

Both Alicia and Mai had saved his life today. 'I'm good, love.'

Gunshots still filled the cavern. Dark patches vied with roaming lights. Drake saw an enemy crawling around the stack of goblets and went to meet him. Mai slipped away. They fought and killed in the darkness, whittling away at their enemy. The piles of treasure rattled and collapsed and exploded as people fought on and around them. In the flaming darkness, the battle seemed to go on forever.

Drake had no idea how many enemy fighters were still in the battle. There was sporadic gunfire now. He counted just two different weapons. One came from behind the pile of rubies, the other from behind a row of chests. But there might be others lying low. Along with his team, he used the shadows to skulk closer and closer.

Mai, a shadow herself, reached one of the men first. She rose at his side, a demon in disguise, and finished him before he could utter a sound. Then she was down and gone, a creeping avenging angel. Dahl used the pile of rubies to confuse his opponent, landing in it and scattering it before reaching over, grabbing the man around the neck and hauling him over the top. As he did so, he broke the neck and left the man sprawling atop the pile of treasure.

Drake waited. The remaining torchlights were now unmoving, some aimed up at where the ceiling might be, others scattered around the walls. He tensed. There was no telling how many of Javier's men still lived, if any. The Ghost Squadron could only scour the dark cavern as best they could.

He rose cautiously, the whole team moving from pile to pile. They walked and sneaked carefully among the riches, checking the dead, looking for the living. Drake and Alicia stalked the darkness together, treading warily. They came across many dead bodies and collected more weapons than they needed to.

But they didn't come across any more still-living enemies.

Drake finally called Kerry forward with their own flashlights. They positioned people well enough so the entire cavern was illuminated and gasped at the sight of the incredible riches. This would go down as one of the greatest finds in history.

Kerry and James spent their time among the riches. Even Danielle was awestruck. Lee eyed the dead bodies and shivered. That could so easily have been him.

Drake pulled Kerry over to him. 'What's the next stage in all this?'

'We have to establish ownership. Someone needs to take responsibility for all this stuff, and maybe there'll be a reward. You could be part of that.'

Drake nodded. 'Then I guess we should get back to the nearest big town and start it all up.'

'That would be a good idea.'

Drake smiled as Alicia came close. 'Thanks for the save.'

'Always wanted to throw a sword into someone's head.'

'Worked out well then.'

'For both of us.'

The team gathered at the foot of all the treasures. They were bruised and tired. Pale torchlight mixed with the burnished colours of the ice cave and the reflections from the treasures fell across their faces. Drake was just glad to see everyone in one piece.

'Is that job done?' Dahl asked.

Drake raised an eyebrow. 'I guess it is. Our second job as part of Spear Solutions.'

'Feels like it lasted months,' Kenzie said, coming up.

'Just days,' Drake wasn't entirely sure. 'Maybe a week.'

Kerry was listening. 'We couldn't have got this far without you.'

As a team, they took several pictures of the immense treasure and then started heading back down the tunnel. Drake wasn't looking forward to the return journey down the glacier, but at least that would be the end of it all. Once they were done, they could let Kerry handle the rest and return home. He didn't always enjoy the end of a mission, but he was quite happy to see the back of this one. It had been fraught with danger and mystery all along, and they'd never been sure where they were going next, or who they would be up against.

Outside, a cool wind blew, but the skies were bright and cloudless.

'Let's get back to civilisation,' Drake said.

CHAPTER FORTY FIVE

They spent one more night in the town.
The hotel was large and luxurious. Drake and the others met Kerry and James, and Jed in the big restaurant and sat down for a celebratory meal. The entire team was seated around a large round table.

Kerry started things off by clinking her glass. 'I propose a toast,' she said, and waited for everyone to charge their glasses.

Drake poured some wine. He sat with one hand gripping his glass and the other on Alicia's knee. Kerry rose to her feet.

'First, to a job well done,' she said. 'We followed the Hellhound scrolls, and we found the Underworld. It was definitely a team effort, though some of our team turned out to be not so friendly. But we overcame that, and we did it.' She took a breath. 'Second, I want to thank Spear Solutions. They kept us safe, they fought for us, they helped locate the treasure and always kept their cool. Here's to the best team in the world.'

She drank. Drake and the others took long sips of their drinks too, and then Kerry sank back into her seat. Dahl was on Drake's right.

'Don't be thinking about putting a hand on *my*

knee,' the Swede nodded pointedly at Drake's other hand. 'I'm not ready for that.'

'I'll try my best not to,' Drake said.

'And don't try telling me it's a Yorkshire tradition. None of that shit. I know enough of them by now.'

'In Yorkshire, we have traditions you can't even imagine.'

'Why doesn't that surprise me?'

Alicia listened idly to the conversation. Mai was on her other side. 'I hear you saved Drakey's life,' she said. 'I'll give you a day off ribbing for that.'

Mai smiled at her. 'Maybe I like the ribbing.'

'Oh, I'm sure you do, one way or another. But I'm gonna give you the evening off. And Mai...' she held the other's eyes. 'Thank you.'

Mai nodded. Kenzie sat to her left. Mai leaned in to her. 'How's it going with you and Dahl?'

Kenzie nodded. 'Pretty good, thanks. He's everything I need.'

Mai smiled and tapped her on the arm. Kenzie turned to her left to see Hayden sat there. 'Thanks for your help today. I needed an assist back in the cavern.'

Hayden nodded. 'No problem. It was wild in there for a while. I thought we were gonna get pinned down. And we fight for each other in this team. That's why it works so well.'

'For one and for all?' Kenzie smiled.

'Something like that.'

Hayden turned to Kinimaka. 'Mano,' she said. 'I'm beginning to think Spear Solutions was the best idea ever.'

The big Hawaiian turned to her. 'The future's

looking good,' he said. 'We can take any job. Anywhere. The world just got a lot smaller.'

'I guess that's one way of looking at it.'

And then Kinimaka rose to his feet. He lifted his glass in another toast. 'To the future,' he said. 'The future of Kerry and James and Jed and of the Cerberim's treasure. And the future of Spear Solutions. Here's to that.'

'The future,' they all said.

And drank from their glasses.

Drake recalled something then and turned to Alicia. 'How are you with all this?' He asked. 'A few days ago you were worried about moving forward, about finding the next thing.'

Alicia smiled at him. 'I decided that Spear Solutions is the way to do that,' she said. 'We never know where we're gonna be next. And that's a form of staying alive, of being in constant motion, of moving on. I think I can live with that.'

Drake felt a great weight lifted from his shoulders. 'Thank god for that,' he said.

The party was just getting started.

THE END

The Hellhound Scrolls

Thank you for reading the latest Matt Drake novel. I do hope you enjoyed it and also enjoyed the general change of direction. I like the fact that we can take the series anywhere now with the new agency. It certainly has opened up the possibilities. Who knows what might happen to the team next?! The next release should be some time in May. Until then, be good and stay safe!

If you enjoyed this novel, please leave a review or a rating.

THE HELLHOUND SCROLLS

Other Books by David Leadbeater:

Blood Requiem

The Matt Drake Series
A constantly evolving, action-packed romp based in the escapist action-adventure genre:

The Bones of Odin (Matt Drake #1)
The Blood King Conspiracy (Matt Drake #2)
The Gates of Hell (Matt Drake 3)
The Tomb of the Gods (Matt Drake #4)
Brothers in Arms (Matt Drake #5)
The Swords of Babylon (Matt Drake #6)
Blood Vengeance (Matt Drake #7)
Last Man Standing (Matt Drake #8)
The Plagues of Pandora (Matt Drake #9)
The Lost Kingdom (Matt Drake #10)
The Ghost Ships of Arizona (Matt Drake #11)
The Last Bazaar (Matt Drake #12)
The Edge of Armageddon (Matt Drake #13)
The Treasures of Saint Germain (Matt Drake #14)
Inca Kings (Matt Drake #15)
The Four Corners of the Earth (Matt Drake #16)
The Seven Seals of Egypt (Matt Drake #17)
Weapons of the Gods (Matt Drake #18)
The Blood King Legacy (Matt Drake #19)
Devil's Island (Matt Drake #20)
The Fabergé Heist (Matt Drake #21)
Four Sacred Treasures (Matt Drake #22)
The Sea Rats (Matt Drake #23)

Blood King Takedown (Matt Drake #24)
Devil's Junction (Matt Drake #25)
Voodoo soldiers (Matt Drake #26)
The Carnival of Curiosities (Matt Drake #27)
Theatre of War (Matt Drake #28)
Shattered Spear (Matt Drake #29)
Ghost Squadron (Matt Drake #30)
A Cold Day in Hell (Matt Drake #31)
The Winged Dagger (Matt Drake #32)
Two Minutes to Midnight (Matt Drake #33)
The Devil's Reaper (Matt Drake#34)
The Dark Tsar (Matt Drake #35)

The Alicia Myles Series
Aztec Gold (Alicia Myles #1)
Crusader's Gold (Alicia Myles #2)
Caribbean Gold (Alicia Myles #3)
Chasing Gold (Alicia Myles #4)
Galleon's Gold (Alicia Myles #5)
Hawaiian Gold (Alicia Myles #6)

The Torsten Dahl Thriller Series
Stand Your Ground (Dahl Thriller #1)

The Relic Hunters Series
The Relic Hunters (Relic Hunters #1)
The Atlantis Cipher (Relic Hunters #2)
The Amber Secret (Relic Hunters #3)
The Hostage Diamond (Relic Hunters #4)
The Rocks of Albion (Relic Hunters #5)
The Illuminati Sanctum (Relic Hunters #6)
The Illuminati Endgame (Relic Hunters #7)

The Atlantis Heist (Relic Hunters #8)
The City of a Thousand Ghosts (Relic Hunters #9)
Hierarchy of Madness (Relic Hunters #10)
The Contest (Relic Hunters #11)
The Maestro's Treasure (Relic Hunters #12)

The Joe Mason Series
The Vatican Secret (Joe Mason #1)
The Demon Code (Joe Mason #2)
The Midnight Conspiracy (Joe Mason #3)
The Babylon Plot (Joe Mason #4)
The Traitor's Gold (Joe Mason #5)
The Angel Deception (Joe Mason #6)

The Rogue Series
Rogue (Book One)

The Disavowed Series:
The Razor's Edge (Disavowed #1)
In Harm's Way (Disavowed #2)
Threat Level: Red (Disavowed #3)

The Chosen Few Series
Chosen (The Chosen Trilogy #1)
Guardians (The Chosen Trilogy #2)
Heroes (The Chosen Trilogy #3)

Short Stories
Walking with Ghosts (A short story)
A Whispering of Ghosts (A short story)

All genuine comments are very welcome at:

davidleadbeater2011@hotmail.co.uk

Twitter: @dleadbeater2011

Visit David's website for the latest news and information:
davidleadbeater.com

Printed in Great Britain
by Amazon